McPHEE GRIBBLE/PENGUIN BOOKS

THE NIGHT WE ATE THE SPARROW

Morris Lurie was born in Melbourne, Australia, in 1938, to which city he returned in 1973, following seven years abroad, mostly in England, Denmark, Morocco and Greece. He is married, with two children, and is a frequent visitor to New York.

His stories have appeared in many leading magazines, including *The New Yorker*, *Antaeus* and *The Virginia Quarterly Review* in the USA; *Punch*, *The Times* and the *Telegraph Sunday Magazine* in the UK; and in Australia in *Meanjin*, *Overland* and *The National Times*. They have been much translated and anthologised, and broadcast on the BBC.

ALSO BY MORRIS LURIE

Novels
Rappaport (1966)
The London Jungle Adventures of Charlie Hope (1968)
Rappaport's Revenge (1973)
Flying Home (1978)
Seven Books for Grossman (1983)

Stories
Happy Times (1969)
Inside the Wardrobe (1975)
Running Nicely (1979)
Dirty Friends (1981)
Outrageous Behaviour (1984)

Pieces
The English in Heat (1972)
Hack Work (1977)
Public Secrets (1981)
Snow Jobs (1985)

Plays
Waterman (1979)

For Children
The Twenty-Seventh Annual African Hippopotamus Race (1969)
Arlo the Dandy Lion (1971)
Toby's Millions (1982)
The Story of Imelda, Who Was Small (1984)

THE NIGHT
WE ATE
THE SPARROW

a memoir and
fourteen stories

MORRIS LURIE

McPHEE GRIBBLE/PENGUIN BOOKS

McPhee Gribble Publishers Pty Ltd
66 Cecil Street
Fitzroy, Victoria, 3065, Australia

Penguin Books Australia Ltd,
487 Maroondah Highway, P.O. Box 257
Ringwood, Victoria, 3134, Australia
Penguin Books Ltd,
Harmondsworth, Middlesex, England
Penguin Books,
40 West 23rd Street, New York, N.Y. 10010, U.S.A.
Penguin Books Canada Ltd,
2801 John Street, Markham, Ontario, Canada
Penguin Books (N.Z.) Ltd,
182-190 Wairau Road, Auckland 10, New Zealand

First published by McPhee Gribble Publishers
in association with Penguin Books Australia, 1985
Copyright © Morris Lurie, 1985

Typeset in Bembo by Bookset, Melbourne
Made and printed in Australia by
The Dominion Press–Hedges & Bell

National Library of Australia
Cataloguing-in-Publication data

Lurie, Morris, 1938–
The Night We Ate The Sparrow.
ISBN 0 14 008864 4.
I. Title.
A823'.3

To Barret Reid
because he doesn't like short stories
and to Philip Jones
because he does

Grateful acknowledgement is made to the magazines in which these stories first appeared:

'A Partial Portrait of My Father, His Birthdays, My Gifts, Bottled in Bond' in *The Australian*; 'Kicking On' in *The Australian Literary Review*; 'Lessons' and 'Were They Pretty?' in *Australian Penthouse*; 'Kelso's Lady' in *Australian Playboy*; 'Camille Pissaro 1830–1903' in *Australian Short Stories*; 'Losing Things' in *The Bulletin Literary Supplement*; 'Rewards' in *Good Weekend*; 'Architecture' in *Meanjin*; 'Tell Me What You Want' in *Nation Review*; 'Swallows' in *The National Times*; 'The Night We Ate the Sparrow' in *Overland*; 'Two Artists' in *Tabloid Story*; 'Letter' and 'Russian Boxes' in *The Telegraph Sunday Magazine*, London.

'Tell Me What You Want' also appeared, in somewhat different form, as a chapter in my novel *Flying Home*.

It is my pleasure to acknowledge the assistance given to me by the Literature Board of the Australia Council.

CONTENTS

LESSONS

MY FATHER MARRIED FOUR TIMES. AND FOUR times was divorced. His first was Ann, followed by Bettina, and then came Clarissa, and after her, Diane. Diane is my mother. And he had elected a fifth, Evangeline, had her in the wings waiting to be brought on stage, the way he always did – we all knew about Evangeline – when he died. He was poisoned. There was no inquiry or autopsy – the story given out was a bad oyster – and in the faded hotel dining-room where they meet once a month, the four wives, they sit not like murderers but like weeping clouds forever mourning that brilliant sun that gave them sparkle and life. Gentle women, pastel hued. As Evangeline is, too. She sits with them, weeping as much or more as the genuine wives. They made a mistake. They shouldn't have done it. They can't understand what got into them. They shake their heads. Their pale hands tremble. You can see the pulse beating in their thin, transparent throats. None has remarried, and not one of them ever will. Their lives in that regard are over. They are clouds. While my father, I know, lies rutting in the pastures of heaven, divorced of one angel, married to a second, polishing a third.

But I wouldn't want you to think that he was a rascal, a rogue, some duplicitous coarse monster unfeelingly laying waste to fickle hearts all around, although, yes, he was a big man, massively-shouldered, burly all over, and I can still feel the warmth of his huge hand cradling my chin, patting my cheek, that hand that was practically the size of my whole face. His shoes – he kicked them off as soon as he came home – were like abandoned boats. He wore the biggest shirts and still they tore at the buttons. And his hats. I was always in awe of the immensity of his hats. But a monster, a rogue? I remember when my mother found out about Evangeline. 'You've been seeing another woman!' she shouted. He didn't deny it. He stood in the bedroom like a leaning wardrobe, his vast double-breasted suit jacket hanging open like curtains, his huge head down. 'I know,' he said. 'I'm not putting up with it!' my mother shouted. 'I know,' my father said again, in exactly the same way. There was no surprise in his voice, nor was there any hint of guilt or contrition, though I saw his stockinged toes fidget awkwardly on the carpet. 'I know,' he said, 'I know.' 'I want a divorce!' my mother screamed. 'I know, I know,' my father said, leaning even more, helpless, as he had, I am sure, been helpless when Ann had screamed at him, and then Bettina, and then Clarissa. My mother began to cry. That's when my father cradled my chin, patted my cheek. He was vast, bent over me, a mountain of cascading cloth that I didn't dare climb with my eyes, and he tilted my head back, gently, gently, and made me look. I saw, then, his true helplessness. I was six years old. On that golden carpet with its pattern of corn-blue flowers and my mother's mirrored dressing-table trembling in the corner with its myriad display of preparations and scent.

Twenty years ago.

The old man.

He was an engineer, a famous engineer, world famous, inscribed not just in the literature of the discipline but in every *Who's Who*, a genius, a thinker, sought and re-spected, but what it boiled down to, his engineering genius, was a way of bending a flap he lucked on when he was twenty-three. A flap in a valve, an oil-bath valve. That was his whole accomplishment. The Wilkins Valve. You've heard of it, I'm sure. Look in your motor car. Look in your boat. It's there when you ride up in the elevator to your office, there when you rush through the skies from one glittering continent to another, there on those tranquil Sunday mornings when you go out to mow your lawns. Whatever you do, you're running on my father's luck. The Wilkins Valve. The old man's flap. Oh, but I am not demeaning him. I would be the last to do that. I know how hard he worked. He was always busy, always working, and so what if nothing else he ever did – all those modifications and usurpations – made that kind of a mark? He was famous, he was esteemed, all manner of doors were always open to him, he made pots and pots of money, there was always money and there still is, a river of money – there is even a fortune in locked-up roubles no one has ever bothered going to Moscow to spend – but sometimes I wonder if his life would have been different if he hadn't lucked onto that flap. I mean, the four wives, and a fifth in the wings. I think that, but then, wherever I am, I look up into those eyes (his huge hand cradling my chin) and I know that it would all have been the same. Exactly the same. Money had nothing to do with it. Not the money, not the fame.

He married, the first time, when he was twenty-two, and then again at thirty, and then it was Clarissa at thirty-seven, and I am twenty-six and I have never married. I have never even fallen in love. Or I don't think that I have. I don't know. I am not sure. I see a girl and my heart yearns and beats but then I feel that the moment I declare myself someone else will step out of the wings, and then someone else, and someone else, there will be scenes and screaming and wide-eyed children to chuck under the chin, and I shrink, I crumple, I retreat, I get the hell out of there, burning like a beacon.

I can't tell you how many times this has happened. With Linda, with Sacha, with Genevieve, with Millicent, with Sandra, with Bernice. And then when I turned twenty-six and it happened again – with Amber! with gentle Amber! – I knew what I had to do.

I flew to Kenya. I would talk to Broderick.

There are four of us, four sons, one from each marriage, and Broderick is the one up from me. Clarissa's. I last saw Broderick when I was fourteen, and then only briefly, but we exchange Christmas cards, as I exchange them with all my step-brothers – a courtesy instilled in me by my mother, as it was instilled in them by theirs – and I know that's not much, but I have never felt that we are strangers. Not in any true sense. I mean, how could we be?

The airline hostess smiled at me as I stepped off the plane – a dark girl, a flashing dark – and I knew she smiled at everyone, it was her job, but still I felt singled out and at

once my heart began that yearning and beating, that leaning into love, and I almost fell, going down the steps from
the plane. My face burned. I felt duplicitous, foolish, a
cheat. Oh, I was hopeless, I was getting worse all the time,
worse and worse, and then I looked up – I was crossing the
tarmac – and I saw for the first time the sky of Africa, and
in its immensity I saw salvation, saw it instantly, for what
is duplicity in such a vastness, how can it even exist? My
spirits soared. My body became weightless. I wanted to
dance and sing. And then Broderick stepped forward – a
scaled-down version of my father in crisp drill shirt and
shorts and long white cotton socks – and I knew at once
that I was in trouble.

Broderick is Professor of Economic Agriculture at the
capital university, he holds the Chair, and for two days he
eulogized the wealth of this, his adopted country, the
potential wealth, his voice rising and rising as he listed
crops and manpower and minerals and fuel resources, his
eyes shining with pride, and I didn't and don't doubt the
pride, but that's not why he was in Africa. I was there for
two days – two days and two nights – and why Broderick
had made this his country, his home, was in no way
hidden. It was in the way he moved, the way he sat, the
way he breathed. My step-brother Broderick was in Africa
for the boys.

But how could this be? He had my father's nose, my
father's ears, my father's smile and leaning stance – scaled
down, to be sure, for who could truly duplicate that
massive-shouldered burly bulk? – he was, as I am, my
father's son, and whatever ambiguities reside within me,
there has never been a hint that they seek that direction, so
what had made Broderick like this?

But he was courteous. He was civil. He was more than
polite. He sat me beside him in his Range Rover and drove
me everywhere under that limitless sky, singing the figures

of production and exchange, and I looked where he pointed, and nodded with what I hoped was suitable intelligence when he looked at me, but avoiding his eyes, for under that sheen of pride I knew what I would see. I could almost feel the huge hand under my chin. For Broderick was helpless, as my father had been helpless, and what Broderick's homosexuality was – his houseboy, his students, the gardener's son – was his frantic retreat from the virulence of my father's unruly genes. Our father's genes. I wanted to talk to him about this, or anyway about myself, but of course I didn't, I couldn't, but when we shook hands at the airport I looked into his eyes, fully, for the first real time, as he looked into mine, and there it was, of course, there it was. I felt my father's hand, standing there, on that heat-hazed African tarmac. It was unendurable. I couldn't speak. I could barely breathe. I turned and fled.

I fled to Paris. To Alaistair.

Alaistair is Bettina's son and his Christmas card is always the same – that view of Notre Dame – as is the greeting he prints in that anonymously neat hand on the reverse, but I flew to him with an open heart, flew to his apartment on the Avenue Foch. A maid opened the door. She wore a small white lace-fringed apron, but everything else – her dress, her stockings, her shoes, her eyes, her hair – was black. She was beautiful. She led me into a room, a lofty panelled room with a glass-topped table and eight hard chairs rigidly grouped under a crystal chandelier, told me that Monsieur Wilkins would be with me presently, repeated the perfunctory smile with which she had answered the door, and was gone. I sat down on one of the hard chairs. The view from the windows was into the tops of trees. I wanted a cigarette but there was no ashtray. I looked into the trees. I looked back at the door through which I had come, closed now, and difficult to make out, panelled as were the walls.

Was Alaistair married? Divorced? Were there children? I knew nothing about him, nothing at all. *Joyeux Noel*, his annual card said. And not signed but initialled. A.W. His initials too as characterless as public print. I sat. Ten minutes passed. Fifteen. Silence. Circumspect silence. Had he forgotten? Had he been told? I thought of the maid, that beautiful aproned maid, and my heart began to beat. I stood up. I sat down again. I reinterpreted her perfunctory smile. I looked at my watch. It was twenty-five minutes. This was too much. I had had enough. I stood up again, just as the panelling at the far end of the room – a set of concealed double doors – clicked open and Alaistair came in.

Alaistair is a small man, or has made himself appear so, affected a style of grooming so fastidious – the clipped and brushed moustache, the sheened parted hair – that he looks as tight and contained as a Victorian pin box, but inside is another man. We shook hands and there, inside him, I sensed that burly shadow. 'How was the trip?' Alaistair asked.

We sat on the hard chairs. He didn't offer me coffee. He didn't offer me a drink. I wanted a cigarette more than ever, but I couldn't take them out of my pocket. Alaistair sat very straight with his fingers laced in his lap. The creases in his trousers were like knives. We chatted. Small talk. Alaistair didn't ask why I was in Paris, he asked nothing personal at all. Nor did he ask about Australia, where he was born – where all four sons were born – and where our father is buried, and where I have always lived. He asked, actually, nothing, and I found myself floundering for subjects to raise. Politics? Trade Unions? The price of gold? That dreadful plane crash in Prague a week ago? It was small talk, chat, those noises you make to be courteous, but each time, with each new topic, Alaistair's mouth tightened. His lips took on a plummy look. 'I'm afraid I am not at liberty to converse in that area,' he said. That was politics. 'You'll pardon me if I don't comment.' Trade unions. 'No, no, I'm afraid I can't move into that realm.' The price of gold, the crash in Prague. I looked at his face but there was nothing there. I looked down at my shoes.

Was he a fool? Was he insane? Or was he in some government's employ, high up in Intelligence, secret work? I didn't know. I never would know. I had flown to him with an open heart, and there he sat, as tight as a pin box, locked away behind those primly creased lips. 'I'm terribly sorry, but I can't venture an opinion on that subject,' he said. We shook hands. I walked the streets of Paris.

There were girls everywhere – students, secretaries, mothers, whores – the streets of Paris were alive with their passing, but I walked looking down at my feet. I didn't know where I walked. I came at last to the Seine. Halfway across a bridge there were steps down to a park, a triangle of green in the middle of the river. I stopped. I looked down. I saw a family – a mother, a father, two small children – sitting on a bench beside the grass. The mother wore a bright blue scarf tied loosely about her hair, the man wore a dark business suit, the children – a boy and a girl – were in identical white shirts and red shorts. They were eating. There was a basket of food on the ground by the mother's feet. The green neck of a bottle of wine poked up past a loaf of bread. The children sat quietly. The father was talking to them. They smiled. The mother produced two apples from the basket. It was a scene of calm domesticity, a private life being enacted in the public sun, and I saw myself as that father, happy and at ease, passing his son a horn of fresh bread, I was that father, and these were my children, and this was my wife, and then I saw Alaistair's maid smiling her outwardly perfunctory smile, and my face began to burn, and I had to look away.

So. To Desmond then, to Desmond, the first of my father's sons. I sent a cable advising him of my coming, and the next afternoon I was on a plane for New York.

Desmond greeted me in the nude. He was in the middle of a shower. And then he had to go out. He was late. 'Make yourself at home,' he said, rushing back to the bathroom. 'You're staying here, of course. You'll find your room. Sorry. Have to rush.' I lit a cigarette. Desmond rushed through again, this time elegantly dressed. 'Help yourself to a drink,' he called, making for the front door. 'Whatever you like.' And then he was gone.

He didn't come back that night. I found some eggs in his refrigerator – there was also some caviar but I left that alone – and then I made some coffee. I was tired, I was very tired, but I didn't go straight to bed. I waited for Desmond. The phone rang every twenty minutes until nearly two o'clock, and each time it was a woman, a different woman. I wrote down all their names, and after each one, the time that she had called. At two I made myself a long drink of whiskey and then I went to bed.

What was Desmond? He owned, I knew, a small, classy art gallery, on Fifty-Seventh Street, in the heart of the heart of New York's art world – there were catalogues in stacks all over the apartment – but was his gallery the reason or the excuse for his hectic social life? He was in and out, in and out, for five days we hardly had a moment together. He rushed in for showers, for messages, to change his clothes. The telephone rang and rang – women, always women – but Desmond was never there.

Five days like that – five days and nights – and then

finally Desmond sat down. He had had his shower. The phone wasn't ringing. He had nothing planned for the night. He sat opposite me wearing just a towel and we talked.

I told him everything. How could I not? That thing that I had seen in Broderick, and sensed in Alaistair, was here no longer a shrunken image, a lurking shadow. Desmond is forty-nine years old, his hair is shot through with grey – the hair on his head and on his chest, that massive barrel – and so I told my story not just to Desmond. I confessed it to my naked father.

I told him everything. I told him about Kenya and Paris – my desperate odyssey – I told him about myself. I told him about my father's – our father's – cradling hand. He frowned. He laughed. He jumped up and poured us fresh drinks.

'Listen,' he said, 'this town is full of psychoanalysts and people who go to them and I've met them all and it's all crap. The old man's genes. So, O.K., you've got them, I've got them. I'll tell you this. They've never done me any harm. What's all this guilt stuff? Enjoy yourself. That's what it's all about. Listen, do you want me to phone someone for you, arrange something?'

'Desmond,' I said, 'have you ever been married?'

Desmond brushed the question aside. 'Look,' he said, 'the women here can't give it away. It's coming out of the walls. I love this place. Couldn't live anywhere else.' He leaned forward. There was a sudden intensity in his eyes. 'You know the old man's big mistake?' he said. 'I'll tell you. He married them. He had to marry them.' There was an edge of bitterness in his voice, or did I imagine that? 'Look,' he said, 'you give them a tumble, they're grateful, you go your separate ways. Beautiful.' He smiled. He gulped his drink. 'Are you sure you don't want me to phone someone for you?' he said. 'I've got a couple you'll go crazy about.'

I shook my head and I looked at Desmond and it was on the tip of my tongue to ask him was he happy, had he ever been in love, truly in love, but then I saw how foolish that would be, and more than foolish, presumptuous and ungracious. I was his guest, after all.

I didn't say anything. I sipped my drink. I looked down at Desmond's huge hands. I saw that gentle family in Paris on the Seine. I saw the mirrored bottles on my mother's dressing-table. I saw Alaistair's secret smiling maid.

Desmond rubbed his eyes. 'Hey, I'm bushed,' he said suddenly. He stood up. 'I think I'll go to bed.' And he flicked off his towel and was gone, loping down the hall, my father's body, an exhausted satyr.

I heard him come in the next night, it was around two, and he was not alone. I heard glasses clinking, soft talk, Desmond's laugh, and then footsteps along the hall. They were going to bed. I closed my eyes and tried to make my mind blank. I had had trouble sleeping ever since I had come to New York. Usually I sleep like a top.

My door was closed, of course, but Desmond had left his open, and lying there in the dark I could hear everything. It was impossible not to. You would have had to have been deaf. For the girl or woman Desmond had in his bed was moaning and shrieking and sobbing with passion. She did it without stop. At times she was practically shouting.

I switched on my light. I sat up. I read all the obituary notices in *The New York Times*. I read the sports reports, I read the listings of the Stock Exchange. By the time she had finished there wasn't a word in the entire newspaper that I had left unread. My hands were black with smudged newsprint. I had smoked seven cigarettes.

I slept till ten and when I woke up I thought of her at once but I knew she would be gone, I would never see her, there would never be a face to put with that sound, with those fevered cries, but when I went into the kitchen, there she was. She had red hair and was wearing a short white dress – it was like a tunic – and she was making fresh orange juice, and if she was less than gorgeous I didn't notice. Desmond was in the shower. I heard that thundering cascade of water. I came into the kitchen and the girl looked up.

O my father's unruly genes. All those marriages. All that pain. O that life of endless performance, to audience after audience, those gentle, pastel brides.

'You were faking,' I said.

Her mouth opened – it was a gorgeous mouth – but no words came out.

'I heard you,' I said. 'I was awake. I was awake right through it. You went for forty-two minutes. No one goes for forty-two minutes. You were faking. You're a gorgeous fake.'

Was I saying this? Was this really me? Was this my voice saying these words? I could hear myself saying them, looking at her mouth, her beautiful mouth, which was open, and stayed open, frozen. Her teeth were very small.

I seized her hand and began to shake it. 'Thank you,' I said. 'Thank you, thank you, thank you.' And I was still shaking it, smiling insanely, joyously beaming, and laughing too, laughing at last, when Desmond came in, my naked brother, and stood there, a wet and dripping blinking fool.

TWO ARTISTS

1

AN AMERICAN DEALER WHO WENT TO AFRICA every year, the hinterland, the unknown parts, one year came to a very poor village and in the chief's hut saw, standing in a corner, a carving, a piece of tribal sculpture, an incredibly beautiful thing. The chief was an old man, with many wives, many children and grandchildren naked in the dust. The dealer said he wanted to buy that piece in the corner. The chief smiled. He shook his head. 'I cannot sell that to you,' he said. 'That is very important to us. It is our history, our beliefs. The whole story of my people is in that carving.' The dealer offered the chief a large sum of money, five hundred American dollars. The chief smiled again, and again shook his head. 'You do not understand,' he said. 'It is our past and our future. Without it, we would no longer exist.'

A year later the dealer came again to the village, sat again with the old chief, saw again his many wives and many children and grandchildren naked in the dust, and this time he offered two thousand dollars. He spread the money out in the dust at the chief's feet. And once again the old chief smiled and shook his head and once again explained how the carving was central to the existence of his people, and that to sell it was impossible, inconceivable, without it they would have no life.

The next year the dealer came again and this time he brought dresses and ornaments for the old chief's many wives, clothes and toys for the many children and grand-children, boxes and packages, mirrors, food. 'Now will you sell me the sculpture?' the dealer asked, offering, this time, five thousand dollars. The old chief sat and saw how happy his people were, and he smiled, and he said to the dealer, 'You are a clever man. But I have explained to you, it is impossible, it is the story of my people, not to be able to look at it would be like death.' 'But of course you can look at it,' said the dealer. 'It will not be locked away in some dark vault. It will be where everyone can see it, whenever they so choose,' seeing, as he spoke, the sculp-ture in a glass case in a famous museum, lit from all sides, people endlessly coming and going, looking, marvelling. 'Five thousand American dollars?' said the old chief. 'Yes,' said the dealer. 'And I can look at it whenever I want to?' 'Yes,' said the dealer. 'All right,' said the old chief, and he smiled, and shook hands with the dealer, and the dealer gave him the five thousand dollars, and then the dealer picked up the sculpture, and was almost out of the old chief's hut, when the old chief spoke. 'Wait,' he said, 'I want to look at it now.'

2

'Wait,' said the sculptor. 'I want to look at it now.'

I laughed.

The sculptor leaned forward and refilled my glass. We were drinking Irish Mist.

It was midnight or after.

We had told many stories.

We sat.

There was a sudden sound of sirens – that murderous music of the city – and then again there was silence.

We sat.

I lit a cigarette. I sipped my Irish Mist.

And then the sculptor spoke again.

'Critics,' he said.

Another story?

Yes, it was another story, but only in the sense that everything is a story, or the prelude to a story, or the aftermath of one.

There were three critics in the city, the sculptor said, and if they said yes then you were famous, you were rich, you were in the best collections, the best museums, you were on television, you were on the covers of magazines.

He named them for me, and then the names of the artists to whom they had said yes, while I looked down at my drink and saw the sculptor's words like tangible things plush with Lear Jets and winters in Acapulco and yachts in the Mediterranean and private streams fat with trout. I saw dazzling parties. Glittering openings. Television. International magazines.

Three critics.

Just three.

There was no other way.

Then the sculptor's words went back twenty years, newly arrived in the city, penniless and unknown, years and years like this, but working, making, hammering out each day his versions of truth, rightness, dignity and honour, the work its own reward, and anyhow, being alive.

Six years like that.

And then, one morning, a knock at the door.

There, on the mat, stood a critic.

One of the three.

He came in. He stood. He looked. He saw, he must have seen, the poverty, the hard life. But he had come for art.

He stood, finally, before one piece, a large unbroken piece of metal, stood before it for a long time, looking and looking, one hand to his chin, the other casually free, and the word yes was in the air like a rising sun, like a golden flag, but fluttering, hovering, not yet affixed.

And then the critic spoke, but what came out of his mouth was not the word but others.

'I think,' said the critic, pointing to the sculpture, carefully, indicating the exact place, 'I think that a hole should go through it. Just here.'

And at once the sculptor understood that things were not to be straightforward. That there was a matter of ego involved. That the critic's ego required that he, the critic, should play some part in the process of creation, that the affixing of the golden word was not, for the critic, enough.

A hole.

The critic's finger not quite touching.

There.

But, said the sculptor, boiling inside with outrage, hardly able to contain himself, if he thinks that there

should be a hole there, *he doesn't understand my work at all*.
A hole?
Never!
I sit with the sculptor in his apartment in the city, surrounded by sirens and silence. Has he finished? I stare down at my drink. Years pass. At last I bring myself to look up. The sculptor's face is invisible. It is not there. It is not on television. It is not on the covers of international magazines.

His words tell me of wily African chiefs.
Too late, too late, he drills his hole.
Fourteen years wide of the mark.
Hollow and useless it falls leaden at my feet.

CAMILLE PISSARO
1830-1903

MOSES STANDS WITH HIS BROTHER BEN IN the Hayward Gallery, London. It is the 150th anniversary of the birth of Camille Pissarro, a steely-skied Sunday, windy and wet. Moses is forty-two, grey-bearded, overweight, Ben a clean-shaven ten years younger. Camille Pissarro, a founding member of the School of Impressionism, was born in Charlotte Amalie, the capital of St Thomas in the Virgin Islands, to Franco-Jewish parents, the third of four sons. His father, a prosperous trader, sent him to school in Paris, where Camille early exhibited an artistic bent, but his father would have none of it, and recalled him to St Thomas to work in the family business. And there Camille might well have remained, a humdrum clerk, but for the fortuitous happenstance of one Fritz Melbye, an itinerant Danish painter, who whisked the young man off to Venezuela where they set up a studio and worked together for two years. Pissarro *père* bowed to the inevitable. In 1855, at the age of twenty-five, Camille sailed once again to France, returning to the Virgin Islands only in the canvases he executed during his first year as a painter in Europe. Bloody hell, thinks Moses. What are we doing here?

Moses is plugged into Ben's cassette. 'I don't know about you, Moses,' Ben had said in the foyer, the second they'd stepped inside, 'but I always take the tour.' And before there could be discussion, Ben had plunked down his eighty p. A blinking Moses had stood and watched as his brother was instructed in the use of the cassette equipment, how to wear it, how to fit the earpiece, how to operate the switches, rewind, pause, on and off, Moses's mind suddenly zipping back fifteen years, to that Saturday morning when he had taken Ben into town to buy him an overcoat. This was that year their parents had died, when Moses and Ben were living together, the family house sold, moved into a flat. What Ben had wanted was a cheap army surplus duffel coat, all his friends had them, everyone at school, but Moses wouldn't listen, insisted Ben try on suedes, sheepskins, things with fur collars, all manner of fancy stuff, overdoing like crazy his new parental role but he couldn't stop himself, wanting Ben to have the best, and in the Hayward Gallery, watching his brother being fitted with the cassette tour, Moses had felt an inexplicable prickle. Sadness? Nostalgia? That great mad time forever gone? Whatever, uncomfortable, uneasy, a stab. And to hide it, as was his wont, quickly made a joke. 'Wow, you look gorgeous,' he had said, wiggling his eyebrows Groucho-fashion, his reward from Ben an exasperated frown. Whoops, thought Moses, wrong again. Then the attendant had suggested that he, Moses, for an additional payment of only thirty p., could be plugged into his friend's cassette. 'Friend?' Moses had said. 'What do you mean, friend? He's my brother.' 'You want it or not?' Ben had said. 'Come on, I'll pay.' And slapped down the money – as though that were any consideration – before Moses could speak. Hey, Moses had thought, what's this? What's this aggression? Moses and Ben walked into the gallery side by side, stepping carefully, aswirl with flex. 'Hey, you want to hold hands as well?' Moses had asked. 'Ssh,' Ben had snapped. 'I'm trying to listen.'

Ben has been in England for a year, running the London office of the firm he works for in Sydney, Moses only three days, a lightning business trip. He will be gone in another four. He is staying the week in Ben's Hammersmith flat, hard on the M4, the traffic roaring past in an endless belt, which Moses drowns out with jazz tapes he made up specially and brought for Ben. Cannonball Adderley. Wes Montgomery. Miles and Monk. Ben likes the Beatles and Neil Young and Elton John, but what the hell, Moses thinks, he can listen to that stuff any time, how often does he have me here? Moses stands now, side by side with Ben, regarding a panoramic view of Pontoise, the village where Pissarro first settled, farm houses, trees, ploughed fields on a rounded hill, a dreary painting, Moses thinks, well, ordinary, what's the fuss? and at once thinks of a marvellous joke, a whole routine, a confusion of Pissarro and Picasso, but when he looks quickly across at Ben, all ready to spring into it, he sees that his brother is serious, intent. Oh-oh, thinks Moses, biting his lip. Better not.

Moses has already disgraced himself once this morning. This was when they were about to get into the car, and Moses had suddenly discovered that he didn't have his wallet. He had run back upstairs. No, it wasn't in the flat.

He looked everywhere. Then outside again, maybe he'd dropped it, maybe it was under the car. Moses ran frantically, kicking at leaves, he can't have lost it, it had to be stolen, glaring at Ben as though it were all his fault, finally standing on the stone steps behind the flats that lead down to the Thames, staring at the black waters, money gone, credit cards, hot-eyed and hopeless. And then whoops discovered it in his left trouser pocket, where he always carried it, where it always was. 'Sorry,' he had said to Ben, attempting a smile. And then, as if that hadn't been enough, in the car, sitting beside his brother, his brother the five-miles-a-morning jogger, the health-food fanatic, the vitamin freak, the two nights a week at gym, Moses had taken out and started to light a cigarette.

The cassette informs Moses of Pissarro's attraction to the works of Corot, Courbet and Daubigny, of his meetings with Monet and Guillaimin and Cézanne, of the diagonals, horizontals and verticals he employed in his new compositions, paintings which were praised by the novelist Emile Zola. His use of broad brushstrokes. His interest in tonal nuances. Moses sneaks a look across at Ben, who is completely absorbed, then quickly around the gallery, that is, the small part of it that he can see. God, he thinks, we're going to be here for years.

In 1870 Pissarro fled to London to escape the Franco-Prussian war. He was to remain for a year. 'Monet worked in the parks,' Pissarro later wrote, 'whilst I, living in Lower Norwood, at that time a charming suburb, studied the effects of mist, snow and springtime.' Moses and Ben stand before his famous painting of the Crystal Palace, their attention drawn by the cassette to how all the figures in the painting are walking away, away from the painter, away from the viewer, walking into the heart of the painting, drawing in your eye, and Moses feels suddenly that old stab of guilt, recalling how he sailed away to Europe when he was twenty-six, giving up the flat, leaving Ben with an uncle. Sailed away and was gone for seven years. He's never forgiven me, Moses thinks, looking quickly over at his brother, who just then takes a step forward, eyes narrowed, to examine the detail. Moses, all at once fearful of the flex, hurriedly takes a step forward too. I mean, he thinks, look at the way he snapped at me in the car.

Wait a minute, thinks Moses, it wasn't the cigarette. I mean, not just the cigarette. He was brusque right from the start, right from the minute I arrived. The way he showed me round the flat. This is the way we make coffee. This is how we make toast. Which we don't eat all over the carpet, by the way. That's your plate. When you have a bath, you wipe it out with that rag, O.K.? And I wouldn't mind if you didn't leave the electric towel rail on all night either. Boy, thinks Moses, shaking his head. What a lecture.

Pissarro returns to France. His house has been occupied by soldiers. Only forty paintings are saved of the fifteen hundred he had left behind, twenty years' work. This is in Louveciennes. Pissarro moves back to his beloved Pontoise. The town is changing, becoming rapidly industrial. Pissarro paints the new factories, the markets. He exhibits. He sells nothing. Year after year it is the same. His growing family is often in severe straits. Pissarro's father refuses to help. Well, thinks Moses, sneaking a look over at his brother, don't think I don't know what's going on.

So he's paying me back, Moses thinks. After all these years he's paying me back. Moses ruefully smiles. Well, O.K., he thinks, if it makes him happy. I don't mind. He wants to give me lectures? He wants to be the big boss? Fine. Sure. No skin off my nose. Except, Moses thinks, his smile dropping away, maybe I was a bit of a bully, but was I all that bad? Look, he was just a kid. Practically a baby. Didn't even know how to make a bed, much less how to hang up a pair of pants. So, sure, maybe I lectured him a bit. But who else was going to do it? Who else was there? And listen, Moses continues, we had fun. It was a good time.

During the 1870s and early 80s, the cassette informs Moses, Pissarro worked closely with his friend Cézanne. Inspired by the example of Courbet, they restricted their palettes, brought back their compositions to basic forms, experimented with textures and brushstrokes. Side by side, the two men painted the same views.

'I didn't know Pissarro worked with Cézanne,' Ben says.

'What?' Moses says, caught off balance. But quickly composing himself, nodding, a reassuring smile. 'Oh, sure,' he says. 'Of course.'

Pissarro wrote to his son, Lucien: 'I haven't done much work outdoors this season, the weather was unfavourable, and I am obsessed with a desire to paint figures which are difficult to compose with. I have made some small sketches; when I have resolved the problem in my mind I shall get to work.'

'Isn't that beautiful?' says Ben. It is a painting of a young peasant girl wearing a hat. 'Look at the sun on the skin, the softness.' Ben moves closer to the painting, his eyes intent. 'You can almost feel it,' he says, and Moses, looking across at his brother, feels again that inexplicable stab. He plummets back ten years. He sees himself standing in the hallway in his old house in England, barefoot, shivering in his pyjamas. It is four o'clock in the morning, winter, dark and cold. Ben is half a world away, a thin, eager voice on the other end of the telephone. He is announcing his marriage. And Moses hears himself too, hears his own voice loud and proprietorial, booming in the dark. What? he shouts. Don't do it! For God's sake, Ben, you're too young!

Has he recovered from that marriage? Moses thinks now. Has he got someone else? We haven't spoken about the divorce, about anything like that. Well, I can't ask him. If he wants to tell me, he'll tell me. I knew he was too young. I told him not to do it. What else could I do?

A woman moves to inspect more closely the canvas before which Ben and Moses stand. 'Excuse me,' cries Moses, warding her off with an upraised arm. 'Can't you see we're *joined*?' And just like that Moses is in tears.

Moses stands in confusion, diving for his handkerchief, biting his lip. What's happening? Why all this? 'Isn't that superb?' says Ben, of the large *pointilliste* canvas before which they stand, peasants in an orchard gathering apples from a tree, and Moses turns and looks into Ben's face and feels swamped with anger. He is in an instant rage. *What?* he wants to shout. *Don't you know anything? Can't you see? One minute he's painting like Cézanne, the next it's soppy Renoirs, now he's churning out this damn pointilliste stuff. Where's his own personality? Where's his character?* But he doesn't. He smiles. He nods. 'Sure,' he says. 'Very nice.' And then quickly has to turn away, blinded by further tears.

Moses stands with his brother Ben before the exhibition's final canvas, *The Avenue de l'Opéra, sun on a winter morning 1898*. 'It is very beautiful,' wrote Pissarro to a friend, 'to paint these Paris streets that people have come to call ugly, but which are so silvery, so luminous and vital. They are so different from the *boulevards*. This is completely modern. I show in April.'

I didn't want him, Moses says to himself. I was forced. I had to do it. I never wanted him. I hardly even knew he existed until our parents died. Moses stands hot and red, riven with shame. I'm a liar, he says to himself. That flat wasn't fun. It wasn't a good time. It was like prison. It was like being in jail.

Moses stands silent and bowed while the cassette

informs him of Pissarro's death, in Paris, at the age of seventy-three, and of the people who honoured his name at his funeral. Renoir was there, intones the cassette, and Monet, and Bernard, and Fénéon, and Lecomte, and Mirbeau, and Durand Ruel, and Vollard, and Matisse, Pissarro's fellow painters and friends. Pissarro linked the 19th Century to the 20th, the cassette sums up his life, adding, as coda, how Cézanne, exhibiting in Aix-en-Provence in 1906, signed himself proudly: *Paul Cézanne, pupil of Pissarro.*

'Fantastic,' says Ben. 'That was really fantastic.' He takes a step back, his eyes gleaming. 'Wow,' he says, shaking his head. And now he turns to Moses. He looks at him directly, for the first time this morning, into his eyes. 'Moses, you were terrific,' he says. 'I expected trouble. You know how you are, the jokes, the rubbish. You didn't do any of that. You were terrific. Thank you.'

Moses somehow nods.

Now Ben, smiling, looks around the gallery. 'Oh, there's a bit more upstairs,' he says. 'Prints and drawings.' He turns back to Moses. 'But you're tired,' he says, looking at his brother. 'You've had enough.'

'Tired?' says Moses. 'What are you talking about, tired? Come on,' he says, stepping smartly back in. 'Prints and drawings is the best part.'

WERE THEY PRETTY?

HIS STORY IS WHEN HE WAS SELLING
typewriters door to door. When he was nineteen, he says.
He's a fat man now, a fat man drinking beer in the sun, but
his story is when he was nineteen he was really something.
Good-looking, he says. More than good-looking. A regular Adonis, he says, staring you right in the eye.

His actual words.

'Handgrenade,' he says.

'Cheers.'

He lights a cigarette.

His story is he used to be into sport, into running, into
rowing, into football, into going to gym three, four nights

a week, into swimming. Into nothing but sport, he says, that was my whole life, all I ever did. And then I had that accident. Ruptured spleen.

He drinks.

He puffs.

Sat home, he says. Sat home for six months. Didn't go out once. And not because I couldn't, he says, but because I was suddenly having such a great time. Because I suddenly realized how much I hated it all, had always hated it, the gym, the training, the hours, the whole way it had hold of your life. All that sports talk, nothing but sports talk, all that sporty horsing around. Muscles. Fitness. Condition. Those guys. The way you always had to hang around with those guys.

Smoke from his cigarette makes his small eyes even smaller.

Smoke or something else.

So his story is for the first time in his life he was happy, he was his own man, he was in control, except, of course, he says, he had to do something, he couldn't just continue to sit around.

Saw an ad in the paper. Phoned them up. Went for the interview.

He stubs out his cigarette.

He pokes what he can of his finger into another ring pull.

Still looking at you, his small eyes not going away for a second.

So here's his story. He chooses a suburb. Drives out there. One of those new suburbs, he says, you know, out a bit.

You know those suburbs? he says. You know where I'm talking about? The wife's Volvo in the carport? Imported shrubs in the garden? No shops, no one around? Everything new and shiny and quiet as a tomb?

Valium land, he says.

He gets there about ten, plenty of time for the hubbies to be gone, the kids all at school. Which is how we were told to do it, he says. They ran us through this training course. No point getting there too early. He smiles. Got to give 'em time to settle down.

He's dressed nice, a suit, a clean shirt, a tie, polished shoes. He looks great.

He knocks on his first door.

His story is it was a neat little machine, lot of features, you couldn't beat it for the money, but he didn't sell a single typewriter. Not a one. They weren't interested in typewriters. His story is how he knocked on the door and they said come in and then they screwed him.

I can't tell you how many times, he says.

Those housewives.

His story is how predictable it was, how it was always the same. You knew it was going to happen the minute they asked you to sit down. When it was on the sofa, not on a chair. When they sat down next to you. When they asked you if you wanted a drink.

They always asked you that, he says. Every one of them. Even if it was ten in the morning, they always asked you that. It was always the same. The same words, even. First the words, and then the hand on your crotch.

You raise an eyebrow.

Really? you say.

But his eyes are hard.

Forget your subtlety, he says. Forget your hints. It was always just like that, a hand straight on your crotch.

Just like that, he says.

Every time.

'Handgrenade,' he says, the fat finger pulling.

'Cheers.'

He's lying, of course. Of course he's lying. You only

29

have to look at him. Look at his body. Look at his eyes.

Were they pretty? you ask.

He doesn't hear you. He chooses not to hear you. He ignores your question. Your question is not part of his story. He has no need for it. His eyes tell you that. Look at his eyes.

And don't think there was any let's sit around and share a cigarette afterwards, he says. There was none of that. There was never any of that. You did what you did, you did what they wanted, and when you'd done it, out you went. Straight out the door.

Those housewives, he says. It was really sad. I can't tell you how I felt. Knocking on all those doors carrying that typewriter and every time it was the same, they just wanted to screw you. It was really sad. I did it for a week, a whole week, and it has to be the saddest week I've ever spent in my whole life. I can't tell you.

You look at him.

You look down.

He's lying, of course. Of course he's lying. He is a fat man drinking beer in the sun, ripping open can after can with that fat finger, handgrenade, cheers, and you sit with him out of courtesy, out of politeness, and of course they are pretty. They are beautiful. They are gorgeous. Come in, they say, with their slitted eyes, with their breasts, with their long legs, with their jutting hips, as you go – endlessly, endlessly – from door to door.

KELSO'S LADY

IT WAS DANGEROUS TO TAKE HER ANY-
where. It was insanity. It was madness. It tore him to
pieces. He could hardly breathe. Whip her into a restaurant, say, and nowhere special either, nothing big deal,
nowhere anyone went, in fact the opposite, the dullest
place, utterly ordinary, and the gloomier the better, it
made no difference, straight away she would fly into action, that handsome fellow at the table over there, or that
one by the wall, or that one, that one, that one, there was
always someone, and they didn't have to be handsome
either, the bald one, the fat one, that sleezy number with
the used-car-dealer's face, whoever, whatever, those big

31

deepset wide blue eyes of hers instantly clicking into that helpless, beseeching look, the parted lips, the tilted chin, her whole face shooting out a clear, unmistakable message – oh God – of availability; and at the end of the meal when she excused herself to attend to the necessary, then it was even worse, intolerable, he would have to watch her like a hawk but still she would manage it, of course she did, he knew how she was – it tore him to pieces, he could hardly breathe – exchanging names, slipping out phone numbers, theirs, hers, making her secret little arrangements.

Listen, don't be crazy, Kelso said. It's just a lunch.

Who's crazy? Kelso replied. You've seen her eyes. That questing look.

Big deal, so she looks around a bit, likes to see who's there. Relax.

What's to relax? I'm dead.

He talked to himself a lot, this Kelso. Anywhere. Everywhere. Day and night. In his head was always holding discussions, making conversation, asking questions, this way, that way, mouthing words, sounding things out. Alone, in company, he was not to be stopped. Kelso talked to Kelso. But no aberration here, no simple bad habit, though it may have begun that way. Talking was his work, his life. For this was Norman Kelso, the playwright, celebrated by the critics as writing the liveliest dialogue in the business, sure, his plots maybe a little stagey, a little forced, his characters a touch lumpy here and there, sure, sure, but just listen to those words.

Absolutely, says Kelso, throwing in a hand movement as well. You said it. Never a truer word.

Which is how he met her, how it began.

Because he was Norman Kelso.

Because he was a playwright.

Dr Leonard Greenfeld phoned. Dr Greenfeld of the courts, the pool, the sauna, the everyday Maserati. Lenny.

His great and good friend Lenny the rich society doctor.

'Listen,' said Lenny, after they'd talked about this and that, joked, the usual, blah blah, 'I've got someone wants to meet you.'

'Oh?' said Kelso, antennae rising, instantly wary.

For he was a collector, this great and good friend Dr Leonard Greenfeld. Of paintings, first editions, antiques, fine wines, the usual clichés, as befitted a rich doctor's station and self image. But a collector of more than that, than those. His real collection was otherwise. For this was of painters, poets, novelists, sculptors. (Kelso was his playwright.) A collector, in short, of those possessors of the magic creativity he, Greenfeld, felt himself to lack. And like all collectors, he liked occasionally to exhibit.

'She's writing,' Lenny said, 'trying to write. I told her I knew you.'

Uh–oh, Kelso thought.

Seeing at once, heart sinking, yet another of those legion of eager women, nice, yes, terribly nice, positively charming, eyes shining, oozing admiration, doting on your every wise word, and then you turn to go and they're like a sack of sand sitting on your throat.

'Lenny,' Kelso said, 'I don't need –'

'Shut up,' Greenfeld said, his voice instantly turning from friend to doctor. 'You know the trouble with you, Kelso, why your plays are so lousy? You don't meet enough people!'

'Hey, thanks,' Kelso said.

'I mean it,' the doctor barked.

'Great,' Kelso bounced back.

'Aw, come on,' Lenny said. 'Don't be like that. Look, you home Sunday, Sunday afternoon?'

'Well, I don't know,' Kelso said, watching himself weaken.

'Fine. I'll bring her round then.'

'Lenny,' Kelso said.

'Ah, stop it,' Lenny said. 'She's gorgeous. You'll love her.'

So Greenfeld brought her round. A summer Sunday, windows open, drapes billowing, warm gentle air. This was in the front room, the lounge. Kelso's wife served coffee. There were some other people there too, though to this day Kelso can't recall who they were. She sat on the end of the settee, bare legged, sandals, legs crossed, her head slightly to one side, cupping her chin with her hand, smoking cigarettes. Alert, listening, taking it all in. Whoever was talking, whatever was said. Kelso said ten words to her all afternoon, if that. All he knew was that when she left, the light went out of the room, the house, the day, his life.

But she had left her play. Her playlet. Seven badly-typed thin foolscap pages hammered out with a dead ribbon and stapled together inconveniently in three places along the top. His wife sitting opposite, all their guests gone now, Kelso lit a cigarette, gave it his undivided best critical attention.

It was one scene, a one-actor, a monologue. A woman sits at her dressing-table, brushing her hair. She awaits a lover. It was a new affair. She has never made love to this man before. The play is her thoughts, her desires, her description of how it will be, physically, emotionally, all spoken to her face in the mirror as she brushes her hair. Words, words. Stroke, stroke. She wears a black negligée. The lobes of her ears are touched with scent. The playlet ends with a tap on the door, the woman rising with a rush.

'Hey, this isn't too bad,' Kelso said to his wife.

'Oh?' his wife said, looking slowly up, regarding Kelso

over the top of the glasses she wore when she read. 'Do you think so?'

So she had read it already! Spotted her enemy as quickly as that!

Kelso ducked.

'Well, yeah,' he said, hiding himself quickly in the flimsy pages, a lecturer fumbling for a misplaced quote. 'I mean, I'm not saying it's perfect, but there's a certain feel here, a kind of intuitive thing . . .'

His wife didn't pursue it. Kelso did. Phoned her. Her number at the top of the playlet, together with her name and address, a little clump of single-spaced personal information, the ribbon so dead by now it was almost illegible, but Kelso could read it, Kelso had no trouble.

'Hey, I think it's great,' he said. 'Full of good things. I'm honestly surprised.'

His wife was in the kitchen, preparing dinner.

'Maybe I should come over,' he hurried on. 'Talk to you, go over it . . . not really possible over the phone.'

He went after dinner.

'Won't be long,' he said to his wife, already half out the door.

She was waiting. Offered him whiskey, coffee. They sat down. She lit a cigarette, crossed her legs, tilted her head in that way he already knew by heart. Her face alert, listening, waiting.

Kelso the lecturer, Kelso the authority.

He told her what he liked about her play, what was wonky, who she should read. He listed authors, titles.

She looked helpless.

'Most libraries,' he said. 'Anywhere.'

Her eyes seemed to grow even bigger, deeper.

'O.K., O.K.,' he said, laughing quickly. 'I'll lend you mine.'

So he came again. And again. Dropped in. This book.

That book. Any excuse. And sometimes no excuse at all. Just there. Soft summer nights. Warm gentle air.

She would tell him later that it took exactly two weeks, two weeks from when they met – that Sunday afternoon in his house, brought there by his friend the doctor – and he would shake his head. 'Really?' he would say. 'Just two weeks?' For it seemed to him longer, slower, a much more gradual and careful and calibrated and complicated passing of time, before, finally, one evening in her house, in the front room, by the light of a dim globe shining through parchment, the lamp she used, as she put it, for atmosphere, he ran at last out of words, out of authors, out of titles, and instead took her into his arms.

Two weeks? Just two weeks?

He had never done this kind of thing before.

And looking up, then, that time, that first time, he had happened upon them in a mirror, the heavy antique gold-framed mirror – elaborate with angels and clustered grapes – above the fireplace, had seen himself framed there with her as in a painting, his hands welcoming her breasts tumbling from her opened blouse, her eyes closed, her soft throat catching the parchment light, a Renaissance chiaro-scuro needing only a title, and this he supplied – *Adultery!* – before quickly reburying his astonished face.

Was she gorgeous? Was she truly gorgeous?

She was thirty-three years old (Kelso was thirty-eight), divorced, one child, smoked too many cigarettes, drank too much coffee, slept badly, in the mornings looked battered under those big deepset wide blue eyes, lived in a house of ivied brick behind a high wall in a good street in a best suburb and drove a white Mercedes and had paintings all over the walls including in the second loo a wonderfully audacious explicitly spread nude and said she wasn't rich at

36

all and was always worrying about money – the ivy was pulling down the house, she said, the Mercedes was full of rattles, the paintings were just things by friends – and her hair was black in bushy springs which she wore either to her shoulders loose and swinging or all piled up high in a careless cloud, save for the odd stray tendril, one uncurling before each ear, plus one or two escaped in back, to artfully offset the silken alabaster of her prettily naked nape.

The marriage that failed had been to a politician.

(You would know who if I told you.)

The child, of course, madly spoilt.

A little girl.

Not yet beautiful, but in that special way that great beauties always begin.

Well, said Kelso proudly. Just look at her mother.

Tallish, the mother, pertly breasted, slim hipped, a derriere to celebrate (the only word to describe it was saucy), that lilting, dancing walk.

And all that just the start, the first impression.

Now there were the details.

The way her lips curved.

The line of her throat when she threw back her head, when she laughed.

The movement of her hands, her fingers.

She had long narrow feet with perfect toes and crossing the bone of the inner ankle a tender blue vein that for some unknown reason made him, Kelso, almost weep to see.

Great in jeans.

In skirts.

Tight stuff, loose, she knew how to handle it.

Fabulous even in the old baggy overalls – a tee-shirt under – she watered her garden in, darting from bush to bush, fiendishly impatient, wanting it over with, done, her springy hair tied hard with a scarf.

But was she gorgeous? Was she truly gorgeous?

Kelso was besotted, bedazzled, enslaved and ensnared, couldn't believe his good fortune, in public with her was a mixture of being so proud and the fear of discovery by someone he knew, his whole being singing like a wire in the wind.

Gorgeous? Truly gorgeous?

Kelso was the last person to ask.

The first time he penetrated her – on the carpet, on the floor – her pupils slipped away upwards to be replaced by two white crescent moons of rapture. And then she drove him urgently home – further, firmly! – with the tucked-up heel of her long narrow adorable right foot.

Nothing like this had ever happened to him before.

Nothing in his whole life.

So Kelso enrolled in that curriculum of lies and deception, stolen phonecalls, cherished moments, falsehood and pounding heart, anxiety and joy, that is the regular course of the married man's affair.

He saw her every day, had to see her every day, or anyway tried to, and if not in person then at least her voice, the sound of her voice. 'Hello?' he would say softly, standing in the hallway at home, one eye out the window, poised to hang up. (Kelso's wife was a schoolteacher, with a schoolteacher's regular hours, but you never know.)

Public phones were safer. There was one at the corner. Another up the street. He used them both, but felt just as jumpy. What if his wife drove past, what story could he concoct, what was he doing in a public phone booth?

But he had to. He couldn't stop. It was as though he had no say in the matter. He was powerless. It was outside his control. Trotting up to the corner shop to buy milk – his wife waiting with the coffee at home – he would eye the phone there and feverishly debate could he risk a moment, did he dare, just a quick call, just to say hello.

And he had, in all probability, already spoken to her that day, probably seen her too, maybe even been in her bed.

It was madness.

It was insanity.

And the number of times he drove there too, without prior arrangement, just on the offchance she'd be home. (She did part-time work in an office, went shopping, went to see her parents, friends, had to take her child to and from school.) And when she wasn't there, which was usual, he would wait ten minutes, which would become twenty, thirty, two hours, and when she finally appeared, they might only have ten minutes together, if that, a cup of coffee, if he was lucky, a couple of words, but the next day, the day after, he'd do it again.

Their regular day was Thursday, Thursday afternoon. He'd take her to lunch first, an early lunch, twelve o'clock, over by one-thirty, two at the latest, then it was into her bed, a Queen-size brass-bedsteaded affair with matching apricot pillows and sheets, from which she would leap at three o'clock, throw on her clothes, a slash of lipstick, tear a comb through her impossible hair – 'God, I must look awful!' – and then into the white Mercedes, gravel scattering as she took off down the drive, to fetch from school her waiting, neglected, poor little girl.

But you want to know how she was in bed, how it was between those silky apricot sheets.

Kelso counted the days from Thursday to Thursday, the hours, the minutes, his mind in endless rehearsal and re-play, endlessly undressing her (though in real life she preferred to do most of that herself), and then holding her, adoring her, the touch of her skin, standing together, bending, kneeling, doing all those special things she liked, he liked, the ways they had got used to, the ways he so far had never dared.

Waiting for Thursday.

Interminable torture.

A flash of heaven.

Then torture again.

Which is not to say there were not other times too –
Kelso ever hopeful, ever alert.

His pal Lenny had to go interstate, would be away a
week. 'Take the car,' he said to Kelso. 'It's about time you
had a bit of joy in your life.' (Kelso's car a battered Volkswagen.)

So here is Kelso, desperate for adultery, burning with
desire, in charge of a fabulous Maserati. What an oppor-
tunity! What a chance!

His wife comes home from her teaching. 'Good day?'
she asks. 'Rotten,' says Kelso, eyes averted, glowering at
the floor. 'Oh, I'm sorry,' his wife says. Kelso stomps off
and pours himself a whiskey, drinks it hunch-shouldered,
turned angrily away.

He is surly during dinner too, and then afterwards,
when he and his wife sit in the front room, as is their
nightly habit, quietly reading, he suddenly flings his book
down, stands, sits, stands again, a scowling, caged beast.

It is an act, of course, a setting of mood for the scene
about to be played. For see how Kelso's wife now looks
up, her eyes soft with concern and sympathy and under-
standing. 'Why don't you go for a drive?' she says. 'You
haven't been out of the house all day, that's what's wrong
with you. Take Lenny's car. Go on,' she urges, 'it's what
you need, it'll do you good.'

He makes a fuss, of course, says what's the point, but
finally allows himself to be persuaded, well, yes, maybe a
long drive somewhere in the Maserati will wake him up a
bit, shake the dust out, yes, why not, worth a try, and then
he listens to his wife's suggestion that he drive to the
ocean, which is a good hundred miles there and back, but

what's that in a car like this? Well, O.K., he says, I might do that. I'll probably be asleep by the time you get back, his wife says. Kelso nods, looking for the keys, eyes down, still in his act of grouchiness and bad mood. Drive carefully, his wife says, as out the door goes Kelso, and twenty minutes later, as had been arranged this afternoon, is between those apricot sheets, and no need to rush home for hours and hours, oh smart fellow Kelso, unlimited time, unlimited bliss.

But her plays, her playwriting, what of that? Which, after all, was why she had gone to him, why they had met, the start of it all. It was a year now, a full year, and what exactly had she written?

Well, she had so little time. She was so busy. Her job, her parents, her little girl. She had things on her mind. She worried. The school fees, the car, the house. And she was tired, she was always so tired. She slept badly, hardly slept at all. Look how battered she was under the eyes.

She managed a page sometimes, an outline of a scene, half a scene, but nothing of significance, nothing at all. Kelso saw that her playwriting, much though she might have liked to do it, was a fiction. It would never happen. It would never take place.

But he did nothing, said nothing, didn't utter a single reproachful word. Somehow didn't care. Why? Was he frightened of her? Ah, come on, Kelso. But he had to acknowledge it. Yes, he was. He was frightened of being sent away.

So he brought her books, as before. Talked to her about plays, playwrights, different ways of doing it, different styles. And when she sagged, rubbed her tired eyes, lit yet another cigarette, said it was hopeless, said she had no talent, said she would never get anything done, he would laugh, he would reassure her, he would tell her to relax, it would all happen, it would all be O.K. For those short moments even believing it himself.

But it was a disappointment. It shouldn't have been that way. It made him feel bad, for reasons he couldn't quite fathom.

Because he wanted a beautiful protégé, beautiful and successful, publicly acknowledging her debt?

For God's sake, Kelso, Kelso told himself, you don't need that kind of ego trip.

No, said Kelso, no, I don't suppose I do.

However, other things now began to impinge. Faintly at first, mere prickles, even less, the shadow of a butterfly between him and the light, but then more insistent, harder, clearer.

The subject came up – Kelso talking about a pal in New York, a frantic womaniser – of three in a bed. 'I just got this letter from him,' Kelso said. 'Absolutely amazing.' He laughed. 'Those Americans. They're such children. They don't know what they're about.' And then noticed a certain look on her face. 'You haven't done that, have you?' he asked. 'Actually, yes,' she said. 'Oh,' Kelso said. He dropped his eyes. He suddenly couldn't look at her. He couldn't speak either.

He didn't know what to say. He was knocked for a loop. He knew, of course, she had been around a bit – a divorcee, after all – but this, well . . .

'With two men or two women?' he finally managed to ask, as though that had anything to do with anything.

'Both,' she said, and when he still wouldn't look at her, reached out and put her hand on his arm. 'Come on,' she said. She looked at him hard. 'Hey, you're really serious, aren't you? You're really shocked.' Kelso tried for a smile but it didn't quite come off. 'Look, it was ages ago,' she said. 'Everyone was doing it. It was that kind of time.'

Well, O.K., sure, it was all a long time ago. It was the politician, that crowd. Forget it. Long gone, long over.

Except suddenly Kelso began to see things, certain things began to appear in a new light.

There was the way she spoke to certain people on the phone. The phone would ring, and she would run off to answer it – she always ran for the phone, never walked – leaving him in the front room, the kitchen, wherever, but he could hear, he could hear how with some people she was open and friendly, with others it was all clipped and full of silences, somehow tense, not her real voice, as though she were talking in code. 'Sorry,' she'd say, when she came back. 'Oh,' he'd say, 'that's all right. Anything important?' And she would shake her head quickly, dismissively, look at him quickly, and then quickly away. 'No,' she would say. 'Just a friend.'

He brooded about that playlet she had given him, those seven badly-typed pages with which, in a sense, she had introduced herself. An affair. A woman waiting to begin an affair. But it wasn't just that. It was an invitation. I am available, it said. I know about affairs. Are you interested? Oh, how professionally done, Kelso thought. How calculated. How cleverly cold.

And that painting in the lavatory, that explicitly spread nude – explicit in everything save for the face, which the artist had oh so cunningly concealed. What was it she had said about her paintings? Oh, just things by friends.

Rubbish, Kelso said to Kelso, stop imagining things.

And when he took her out to lunch and straightaway her eyes were flying all over the room, sending out that helpless, beseeching, clear sexual signal to every man in the place – tearing him to pieces, impossible to breathe – or was he imagining that too?

And then Kelso had to fly to Montreal – they were

43

putting on one of his plays there, it was quite an honour – and he missed her terribly. He was there for two weeks, and then a week in New York, but where before travel had always excited him, delighted him, awakened him anew to the world's possibilities, and his own, extended his limits, redefined his goals, now he saw nothing, felt nothing, wanted only her. In Montreal there was a red-headed Irish poetess he could have had – they had a drink together, during which time she made that abundantly clear – and in New York there was a lady similarly disposed, but both times Kelso said no. No thanks. Thank you very much but no thanks.

For how could he? Every woman he saw reminded him of her, of the way she walked, the way she moved her hands, lit a cigarette, drank coffee, that special way she had of ducking her head, the way she laughed. She was in his pores, in his breathing, in his every moment, awake and asleep. There were women more stunning, more spectacular, different in all manner of ways, but he was not interested, they were not for him. He wanted her. He wanted only her.

And the prickles, the doubts, the suspicions, the strained phonecalls overheard filled with silence, the almost visible face on the explicit nude, all those shadows and terrors that flicked across his shuddering heart?

Vanished in a flash when he knocked on her door and she opened it wearing a pale pink silk peignoir, and she smiled, and opened her arms, and the peignoir opened too, and she welcomed him, welcomed him home.

He loved her, he was insane about her, he couldn't live without her, it was just as it had been before. He lived from Thursday to Thursday, counting the hours, phoning her every day, twice a day, dropping by, dropping in. He would never go away again, he promised himself, no matter what, not if it was without her. He couldn't stand that. It was just too terrible.

One afternoon when he phoned, he suggested that he come around that night. He was desperate to see her. He would find a way. 'I'll tell her I'm going to a movie,' he said. 'I haven't done that for ages.'

There was a pause on the other end of the line, and then what sounded to him like a sigh. 'Look, could we make it another night?' she said. 'Honestly, I have to get some sleep.'

She was not well. She was coughing. It was those damn cigarettes. She could hardly sleep. He had seen her yesterday, just for a few minutes, and around the eyes she had looked particularly battered.

'Well, O.K., sure, I understand,' Kelso said, 'it's just that I so much wanted to see you.'

'I want to see you too,' she said, 'but if I don't have a decent night's sleep tonight . . .'

He understood. He would call her in the morning. Be well, he said. Sleep well. It's all that coffee and cigarettes. I love you, he said. Call you tomorrow.

He couldn't see her, but he couldn't stay home that night either. He was too jumpy, too edgy. He needed to do something, see someone. He had to get out of the house.

He phoned a friend. He would go over there. They would play a few jazz records, drink some whiskey, talk a bit, kid around. He was not a bad guy, this friend, and too much time had slipped past since Kelso had seen him last.

It was a great evening, just what Kelso had needed, and it was sometime after one when he decided to call it quits. He went out to the car, sniffing the night air grandly, looking up at the stars. He had had a lot of whiskey but it hadn't seemed to have done anything serious to him. His head felt very clear. He waved to his friend, put the car into gear and began to drive home, and it was only when he was more than halfway home that he decided – what the hell – to do a long, looping detour and drive past her house.

What for? He didn't know. He didn't have the faintest idea. It was just a thing he felt like doing, a thing that he wanted to do. When he turned into her street it was all very quiet – dark houses, dark trees – and when he was still some distance away he saw a car parked by her house and he slowed down, and as he went slowly past he looked up the drive and saw that there was a light on upstairs, in her bedroom, the soft light that she had by her bed, and a downstairs light too, the light over the front door, the light she switched on for guests.

Kelso drove home, sick to his stomach, aghast, bewildered, awash with tears. He could hardly see to drive, they streamed so from his eyes. But somehow he did, and parked in the street, and then just sat there, behind the wheel, not moving, not able to move.

Oh the bitch, the slut, the prostitute, the rich society whore. It was all true. Everything he'd dreaded, everything he'd tried to ignore. Three in a bed. Orgies. Endless affairs. Oh yes, she was that nude in the lavatory all right, the slut, the shameless slut.

And I loved her, Kelso said, hammering with pain.

The tears flooded from his eyes, flooded and streamed. He wiped them rudely with the back of his hand.

He lit and smoked a rare cigarette. Then lit and smoked a second, a third. The car filled with smoke. Kelso sat.

Maybe it was just a doctor, Kelso offered. Maybe she's ill.

Come on, said Kelso.

I should have stopped, Kelso said. I should have got out, at least had a proper look at the car.

Come on, said Kelso.

Kelso, sick to his stomach, sat and wept. He couldn't stop it. It was like acid inside, waves, a searing pain.

An hour like that, an hour and more.

And now at last Kelso spoke to Kelso.

You know why you drove past there tonight, don't you?

Yes, Kelso whispered.

You knew what you'd see.

Yes, Kelso said.

So you wanted that, you must have wanted that.

I don't know, Kelso said.

Kelso!

Yes, Kelso said. Yes. I did.

He bowed his head. The tears fell unimpeded now, fell to his hands, where they lay in his lap.

O.K., said Kelso, O.K. That's enough now. That'll do. Blow your nose. Wipe your face. You don't need all those tears.

Kelso blew, wiped, blew again.

Better? Kelso asked.

Yes, said Kelso.

Good. Now go inside. Go inside to your wife.

A PARTIAL PORTRAIT OF MY FATHER, HIS BIRTHDAYS, MY GIFTS, BOTTLED IN BOND

MY FATHER WAS A TALL MAN WITH CRAGGY features, tufted eyebrows, the lines of practised bonhomie etched deep as gullies down his face – oh he knew how to smile – and of course I loved him dearly but I could never remember his birthday. Not once. Not a single time. Year after year it was always the same. I don't know why. And birthdays were so important to him. He loved them. He loved the fuss, the ritual, the giving and getting, the whole business of gifts. He lived for birthdays. He needed them. He adored them. But in all those years that he was alive – it's fourteen years now since he died, fourteen years this March – I never remembered, not a single time, not once.

But if I forgot his, he never forgot mine. A pony at eight, a Porsche at eighteen, the years around and between no less lavish and splendid. The last gift he gave me was a Mercedes. This was on my thirtieth. We were having dinner at the house, as we always did on my birthday. He handed me a little box, sumptuously wrapped, done up with a huge silk ribbon. The key to the Mercedes was inside, but I didn't know that then, I didn't know that for some time, for before I could get round to opening it – there were other gifts, we were drinking champagne – he excused himself from the table, excused himself to go to the bathroom, and that's where we found him, all properly belted and buttoned and zipped, just as he'd left us, peacefully sitting, slightly sloped against one wall, as though he'd just sat down for a little rest, the only apparent difference those lines of practised bonhomie that etched his craggy features relaxed at last.

That was fourteen years ago, as I've said, and from that day to this his birthday has been etched on my mind as firmly as those lines that folded his face – etched like a point of light to which the year inexorably moves, the hub, the nub, the pinnacle and peak, the year's rightful climax, the next year's proper beginning. Since he died there hasn't been a single year in which I haven't remembered, whatever I was doing, no matter where I was.

Impossible to forget now, indelibly inscribed.

The seventeenth of September.

My father's birthday.

But of course I didn't need to remember, when he was alive.

I recall, for instance, that year when I was nineteen – but it could as well be any of the others. Year after year it was always the same. But nineteen bears the specialness of being the last year I lived at home, though I came back all the time, stayed overnight, weekends, brought my new bride, my three children as each was born, was always coming back to the big house with its white flagpole in the vast front lawn and the clock tower against the dark trees and the tennis courts and putting green and the high airy stables (later converted to a massive garage) and the view of the sea, was forever coming back for all sorts of reasons but especially for birthdays, always for birthdays, his, mine, whoever's, unthinkable not to, a family tradition, year after year.

So then.

That year.

I was at the university then, studying Spanish Literature – Quixote, Marquez – and I got home at five o'clock, five on the dot by the clock in its tower against the dark trees. I climbed out of the Porsche. And there was my mother, standing like a white ghost in the shadows, a finger to her lips. She didn't speak. She didn't need to speak. She didn't need to say a word. The minute I saw the bottle of whiskey I knew at once that it was my father's birthday, that I had forgotten yet again.

King George IV whiskey, unwrapped.

Year after year it was always the same.

I took the bottle, nodded, and went quickly through to the house.

But a word about this whiskey.

My mother's drink was gin – gin and tonic was her preference but if there wasn't any tonic, don't fret, gin with bitters would do just as nicely, thank you very much, or vermouth, or lime juice, or orange juice, whatever was about, gin with anything, really, or just with ice, if that's all there was, or even with nothing, gin on its own. Yes, she liked her gin. But if there was no gin? Right out of gin? Not a drop of gin left in the house? Well, vodka would be just as marvellous, of course. Tequila, akvavit, anything like that. Whiskey. Rum. She liked a nice smooth rum.

She liked her wines too, the reds, the whites, she liked them all, whatever was going, dry, sweet, bubbly, still. The sherries, the ports. Pim's, too, Campari, all the long drinks. She never said no to a cognac either, a brandy, the cordials, the liqueurs. In short, my mother's preference may have been gin but she was perfectly happy with whatever was available, she knew how to accommodate herself to any situation, and did, oh how she did, but my father had one drink and one drink only and that was King George IV.

It was the best, he said. It was the best whiskey there was. It was the only whiskey. Anyone who knew their whiskey knew that. Look at it. Smell it. Taste it. Ah! Nothing, he said, shaking his head, nothing in the whole world came anywhere near King George IV.

How he came by this curious intelligence God only knows – I certainly never did – but he was absolutely steadfast in his belief. For when he died, and we came to sort through the house, tidying and enumerating and cataloguing his many possessions, we found whiskey all over the place. We found whiskey in the stables and under the stairs, in the attic, in the cellar, in the clock tower, in the changing rooms by the tennis courts. We found whiskey in the cupboards, in the wardrobes, under all the beds, pushed here, poked away there, a ransom in whiskey, whiskey galore. We found it by the case and by the half case, single bottles, miniatures, crocks and flasks, gift decanters, Christmas boxes, presentation packs. Every kind of whiskey you could think of was there, Dewar's, Haig, White Horse, Black Douglas, Johnnie Walker – both Red Label and Black – Ballantine's, Bell's, all the blends, the popular brands, Cutty Sark, Teacher's, Black and White, J & B, Vat 69. And then the single malts, the Glenfiddichs, the Glenlivets, there were six lovely bottles of ten-year-old Laphroaig from the Isle of Islay – deep and peaty, liquid smoke. Jameson Irish was there, and three cases of American bourbon – Old Grandad, Wild Turkey, Jack Daniel's Quality Tennessee Sour Mash. There was Canadian whiskey – Canadian Mist, Canadian Club – Japanese whiskey, Australian, Spanish, everything from fire water to heaven on earth. And they were all of them, every single bottle, unopened, untouched, birthday presents and Christmas presents and presents given in the line of business by people who had blundered, who had got it wrong, who hadn't bothered to find out or know or understand my father's singular taste.

I knocked on his door, the door to his study.

'Yes?' he said.

It was the same every year, year after year it was always the same.

He was sitting at his vast desk, fingers laced on the red leather – that vast mahogany desk with its four telephones and the gold and ivory writing set and the monogrammed cedar humidor and the deep crystal ashtray filled each day anew with the finest white sand.

Light from the long window to his right – the dark trees, the view of the sea – fell softly in.

'Happy birthday, Father,' I said, and presented the bottle of whiskey, held it out in my right hand, placed it carefully before him dead centre on the red leather of his vast desk.

'Oh,' he said. 'How kind. Thank you,' he said. 'Thank you very much.'

He picked it up, held it in his huge hand, smiled down at the label, that effortless smile he had, those lines of practised bonhomie.

I smiled, of course, too.

And then we stood – it was the same every year – both smiling, both silent, both looking down at the bottle of whiskey in his hand.

We stood like that, it always seemed to me, for hours.

But at last he sighed, he cleared his throat, he looked quickly up at me, he smiled yet another of his winning, effortless smiles. And then he turned, bottle in hand, to the wall of cupboards behind him, and slid them open, the doors gliding like silk, and I saw – as I saw every year, every year it was the same – his wall of whiskey, his King George IV whiskey, bottle after bottle, a hundred bottles, a thousand, his cache, his supply, floor to ceiling, wall to wall, the whole wall softly alight with that special light, that golden light, falling from the window so softly in. And he found a space, he made a space, and put in my bottle, the bottle I had just given him, this perfect birthday gift from his beloved and attentive and thoughtful son.

SWALLOWS

FOR A TIME IN THE MID-SIXTIES I LIVED IN Tangier. It was a good time to be there. It was an easy place to live. It was like nowhere I had ever been before. And it was cheap. Food was cheap, and so was where I stayed. My room and breakfast were about ten dollars a week. The fatima who came in every day made my room and washed my clothes, and whenever I wanted a hot shower she connected up the gas cylinder in the bathroom – an unwieldly business – and laid out a pile of fresh towels, thick white towels, smelling of sun. There was a slight extra charge for this, but nothing, really, hardly anything at all. Totted up each week it came to perhaps another two dollars. And travel was cheap: the Moroccan buses, the ferry to Gibraltar and Spain. By bus I went to Meknes, to Rabat and Fez. I went to Ceutta, that Spanish town on the Moroccan mainland, and bought Spanish brandy, smoked ham and sausage. And once a week I went to Gibraltar and Spain. The border between them was open then; all you needed was your passport. The formalities were a matter of minutes. You walked across. The ferry to Algeciras left at nine in the morning, was across the Strait in a little over two hours, the one back left at three or four in the afternoon. It was a heady feeling. You had been in three countries in the one day.

Where I lived in Tangier was not exactly a hotel. It was a dozen rooms off both sides of a long cold corridor, where all through the night the tap of high heels reverberated like metronomes on a grand piano. First there would be a buzz at the front door – that clamourous electric buzzer – and then that sound, that tapping. Señor Adolfo, the small, nervously-smiling Spaniard who owned the place, called it a pensione, but of course it wasn't that. The rooms were rented out by the hour. And I was there to lend respectability: writer-in-residence in a house of assignation in Tangier, as I boastfully wrote to friends at home, hardly believing it myself. But it was true. The whores tapped with their heels, I tapped on my portable Olivetti: a household at work.

But my position in Señor Adolfo's pensione was not unique. There was another writer there, too, a tall frail Englishman named Orford St John. Orford had the bearing and manners – the correctness – of an Old Etonian, or anyway of some similar public school, but overlaid with the fussiness of age. He was in his sixties, wispy white haired, a homosexual. He was there when I arrived, had been there for about six months, living in the little room to the left just past the front door, and he welcomed my company. He seemed to have few friends. He showed me around the town, walking stiffly in a huge straw hat. He showed me the markets and bazaars, the cafés, the cheapest places to eat, the places to avoid, he opened up for me the labyrinth of the medina. He pointed out the mosques, the bath-house, the famous places. He knew the history. He had discovered Tangier in the thirties, he told me and now, retired (although I never learnt from what), he had come here to live. He smiled. 'Like an aged spinster eking out her days,' he said. He was not well. He suffered from palpitations of the heart, 'the flutters', as he called them. His hands trembled. On the slightest hill we would have to stop while he caught his breath. Then we would sit down somewhere and order mint tea, blinking and trembling Orford delighting me with the gossip of the town, retailing it with that wonderful maliciousness of someone who has not been invited to the party.

Occasionally we drank a glass or two of white wine together in a small out-of-the-way bar run by another Spaniard, Benito. I would knock on Orford's door around six, and then wait – he always took a long time – while he got himself together. Many times my knock would wake him from an afternoon sleep. He would awake dazed, his wispy hair flying in disarray. 'Ten minutes,' he would call. 'Can you give me ten minutes?' He usually took longer. I would stand in the corridor and wait, listening to him fussing. 'Oh, where are my shoes?' I would hear him crying. 'Oh God, now they've stolen my shoes.' But finally he would emerge, wearing his huge straw hat, even though the sun was going or had already gone down, and together we would walk to Benito's bar. We would sit there for about an hour, on stools, at the counter, drinking our wine, eating the *tapas* that came with it; small plates of olives or fried calamari or grilled anchovies or sardines. An old record player played the same scratchy tunes. There were no windows, there was nothing to look at. Quite often we were the only people there. There were more interesting places to drink, to spend time, but Benito's, even by Tangier's standards, was ridiculously cheap, and Orford, I knew, had to be careful with every penny. God knows what he lived on. He never ate out. He took his meals at Señor Adolfo's, in the small crowded kitchen, with the fatima and Adolfo and Adolfo's boyfriend and Adolfo's mother and occasionally, too, a whore who was down on her luck. A canary chirped in a cage on one wall. A cuckoo clock adorned another. A window looked out on a patch of garden where tethered chickens pecked the hard earth. When the front door buzzed it rang in the kitchen, creating an instant hullabaloo, the canary fluttering, Adolfo springing nervously to his feet. The air was always steamy, potatoes on the boil. Orford ate there silently, rarely saying a word. He ate what was put in front of him, with a polite nod of his head. He had no option. It was what he could afford. His only indulgence was to go to Spain once a month, where he went to see a friend. But it wasn't just the money, why we drank at Benito's, hidden away from café life, the promenading, the faces, the gossip and news. Orford felt himself a failure. He didn't like to be on view.

I asked Orford one evening, when we were sitting in Benito's, had he noticed that our two patrons bore the names of the century's greatest fascists. Orford laughed. He was delighted. 'I think I'll put that in my play,' he said.

Orford was only recently a writer. He was beginning with a play. He hoped to emulate the style of Noel Coward, whose work he adored. Noel Coward was his idol. Noel Coward was 'The Master', the beacon to follow. Orford's play was set in a grand English country house, the home of a titled family, and in the first act the debutante daughter gave birth to a black child. Orford wasn't sure what happened after that, in the next two acts. He hadn't worked that out yet. 'Don't worry,' he said, 'it'll write itself. All I need is the momentum.' Meanwhile, he was 'blocking in', as he put it, the first act. He showed me his first pages. 'I know, I know,' he said, 'I can't do dialogue, but don't you think the structure is fine?' Orford chuckled with evil delight. 'Oh, I can just see their faces,' he said. Whose faces? The debutante's titled parents? The stunned audience in a London theatre? I bent over Orford's pages, prolonging the moment when I would have to look up. I didn't know what to say.

We would collaborate. I, as a published writer (one short story, an accepted but yet-to-be-published first novel), would handle the dialogue. Orford would furnish the correct nuances of upper-class English life. Together we would evolve the plot, heedful of the example of 'The Master'. Orford was very excited. There was a lot to discuss. We sat in Madame Porte's Salon de Thé, where the old French of Tangier passed their afternoons, with its potted palms and white-aproned waitresses and trays of delicate patisserie. Classical music played softly through hidden speakers. I ordered coffee, Orford, fearful of his heart, tea. We selected our cakes. We talked. We laughed. We concocted the wildest turns. Orford's hands trembled, his whole face trembled. His usually pale cheeks flushed red. We scribbled notes, characters' names. I knew it would never happen, I think we both knew that, but it didn't matter. That wasn't the important thing. When the bill came Orford attempted to pay but I wouldn't allow it. 'It's all right, Orford,' I said. 'You can pay me back when you're rich.' 'We'll both be rich,' Orford said.

The following afternoon Orford suggested, for the first time, that I might like to meet one of his friends. We set off together to see Miss Mitchell.

I have said that Orford seemed to have few friends, and

certainly no one ever came to visit him in his room at Señor Adolfo's, but there were three or four. In time I was to meet them all, those English widows and spinsters of Orford's generation. One painted. Another wrote teenage romances for a British publisher. A third tended her garden. They all kept busy. They filled their days. They gossiped. They knew all the news. They rushed about the markets with their straw shopping bags, strident and boisterous. They had lived in Tangier for years, they knew it backwards. But why were they there? Some sexual proclivity? Lack of funds? Did they pine for England, dream of one day returning? I didn't ask, I felt it too rude to ask, and if I seemed to see in their busy eyes the sadness of exile, was it really there, or did I force it upon them for my own needs? They were strange ladies, noisy, leathery with sun. And Miss Mitchell – Gladys – was the strangest.

Miss Mitchell's life was dogs and cats. Dogs and cats were her whole life. When Orford unlatched the gate to her garden, dogs flew at us from all directions, yelping and barking, mongrels, mutts, curs, dogs of every shape and size, a huge brown boxer, a torn-eared alsatian. I was terrified. I didn't dare move. I couldn't even speak. Then Miss Mitchell appeared, running from the house, waving a stick. 'Oh, stop it, dogs!' she cried. 'Stop it at once! Can't you see they're friends?'

She led us to the house, swiping with the stick, a small woman, harried, exhausted, but with a kind face, a kind English face. She could have been a librarian, a lady serving in a village shop. 'Shoo!' she cried. 'Go away, dogs! Not now!' Orford walked stiffly, holding carefully the box of cakes he had brought for our afternoon tea. The garden was a wasteland, the ground everywhere dug up, a few tattered shrubs. Chickens scuffled in a wire pen. A cocka- too hopped on a chain. The house was old, dilapidated, the wooden walls brown with dust. We came in through the kitchen. I thought I was going to be sick.

It was the smell, a rank airless stench of animals that filled the house like a plague. It was everywhere. It was in the furniture. It was in the walls. I could feel it in my eyes. 'I know, I know,' Orford said to me softly. 'You get used to it.' 'I'll be with you in a minute,' Miss Mitchell said. 'I just have to feed the cats.'

There were twenty of them, twenty and more, on every horizontal surface in the kitchen: on the table, the shelves, the cupboards, the floor. Miss Mitchell put a huge black kettle on to boil. It was like a signal. The cats began to prowl, pushing at one another, pushing at her. She tore up loaves of bread. The cats became more insistent, pushing harder, growling. When she began to open tins of sardines they leapt at her hands. Miss Mitchell spun this way and that, fending them off with her elbows. It was like some maddened choreography. She mashed the bread and sardines with her fingers, dolloped it out into twenty tins, poured on hot water. The cats were now in a frenzy. She barely had time to stand back. The cats flew. It was all over in less than a minute. Miss Mitchell rubbed a hand over her eyes. She stood like that for what seemed a long time. Then she took a deep breath. 'The tea,' she said. 'The tea.'

I sat with Orford in the sitting room. The smell here was even worse. I was certain I was going to be sick. But it was more than just the smell. It was the bare floorboards, the walls as brown with dust as those outside, the scratched and filthy doors. And more than that. Everywhere, on the walls, on the mantlepiece over the empty fireplace, on the window ledge, on the rickety table in the middle of the room, on the floor, were china dogs, plastic cats, saccharine rhymes to 'Dear Doggie' and 'Darling Pussy' on hung-up tea towels, yellowing calendars with collies and black and white terriers, postcards, cheap paintings: a Woolworths of cloying pet-lover bric-a-brac. In the poverty of the room it was nauseous and heartbreaking. 'Poor soul,' said Orford. 'She's got no money. Everything goes on those stupid beasts. That's why I always bring these cakes when I come. They're probably the only thing she'll eat all day.' He looked quickly at the kitchen. 'Which she'll try to give to *them*, if I don't watch her.'

Miss Mitchell brought in the tea, three cracked cups on a tin tray. Orford opened the box of cakes. I shook my head, no, not for me. I couldn't eat anything. I couldn't even touch my tea. The idea of eating anything here, in this smell, was unthinkable. I looked at Miss Mitchell in her torn cardigan and her dirty cotton dress and her toes pushing out of her shoes – old cracked shoes with the laces gone – and I tried to smile as she sighed and said what a bother it was now that Harold, that was the boxer, could open the bedroom door, which is where she had to put him because he fought with the alsatian, and two other dogs had to be locked up too, more fighters, in separate rooms, and it was God's own business to remember who was where and who'd been fed and exercised and who hadn't, and yesterday the neighbourhood boys had brought her another dog, poor little thing, they'd found it abandoned. 'Just thrown away!' Miss Mitchell cried, her eyes flaring with outrage. She was on the brink of tears. 'Well, they always know they can bring them here,' she said. 'I'll look after them.' 'Come on, Gladys,' Orford said. 'Eat your cakes, there's a dear.'

She would die. She would die of exhaustion. She would starve to death. In my room at Señor Adolfo's I stared at my typewriter. The front door buzzed, the whores tapped, the canary in the kitchen fluttered in its cage. Orford, in his room, scribbled his country house play. I stared at my typewriter. I could see it all. I could see it exactly. It could be happening now, this very minute. Her heart would give out. She would fall to the floor. The cats would prowl over her body, pushing and growling. The dogs would howl to be fed. They would break out of their rooms, maddened with hunger. They would savage her. They would tear her to pieces. No one would miss her. Days would pass. And what was left would be found by Orford, poor Orford, come to call, with his kindness, with his box of cakes.

I had arrived in Tangier in January, that month of rains, and now it was April. The days were sunny, and each day hotter than the one before. The heats of high summer, of August, were already in the wings. I spent less and less time in my room. My window was on the wrong side for the sun. On even the brightest days it barely penetrated. There was always a feeling of damp. The view of palm trees and blue sky was like a taunt. I felt constrained. There seemed nowhere to move. The table I sat at, read at, wrote at was less than a pace from the bed. A bulky wardrobe loomed from the opposite wall. Where before I had spent each morning there, now I went out. I sat in the cafés, drinking *café con lèche*, smoking. I watched the passing faces, the locals, the regulars, the tourists. I walked. I made friends: a Canadian, a New Yorker, a fellow Australian. In a market I bargained for and bought a rug, and then wondered why. Where would I put it? It lay rolled up on top of the wardrobe, its wonderful colours hidden away, bound up with string. I seemed to see less and less of Orford, too. I lived in dread of it, but there was no talk of our play. When we sat in Benito's together, we sat mostly in silence, listening to those scratchy tunes. Passing Orford's door each morning I began to notice what I hadn't before, or had chosen not to: each morning an empty bottle of wine. '*Si, si,*' said Señor Adolfo, sadly shaking his head. *'Barrachio.'*

Was it time to leave, to move on? Should I return to London? I sat in a terraced garden overlooking the Straits. Boats like toys moved to and fro, tracing white wakes in the blue water. The sun shone down. The air was as clear as glass. I could see Spanish roads, rooftops, a village square. I thought of the bookshops in Charing Cross Road, the cinemas in Leicester Square, the solid reassurance of the Sunday papers, the Rembrandts in the National Gallery, the Picassos in the Tate. I sipped my mint tea. I lit another cigarette. Moroccan music droned in the afternoon. Or should I go somewhere new; Paris, Finland, Berlin?

No. I hadn't finished with Tangier. I loved it. It was so easy. It was still so endlessly different. I loved the Socco Grande and the Socco Chico, the crowded narrow streets, the smells, the cake seller with his tray buzzing with bees. A little man sold scissors. 'Very good, cheap,' he cried, clicking them over his head. I ate chicken and cous-cous in Moroccan restaurants tucked away in the medina, finished the meal with a wedge of watermelon, went somewhere else for coffee, to sit, to talk. I walked on the wide beaches. I sat in gardens. I strode along dusty roads in the hills. There was a man who sold hedgehogs. When you asked to see one he showed you an empty hand. Then – a wink, a smile – a hedgehog appeared, crawled out from his wide jellaba sleeve.

I sold another short story, my second. Fifty pounds minus my agent's commission in London was nothing at all; here I felt splendidly rich. I celebrated in a French restaurant. I bought a silk shirt, goatskin sandals, had my hair cut, had my photograph taken in the Socco Grande against a backdrop of veiled fatimas and rusty buses and rushing boys. I planned a trip to Casablanca and Marrakesh.

One afternoon on the ferry from Gibraltar, my weekly

trip, a Moroccan in a business suit engaged me in conversation. We stood together on the deck, the bare hills of Africa across the water aged and golden in afternoon sun. He smiled. He offered me a cigarette. He asked where I lived in Tangier, how long had I been there, how much longer did I plan to stay. I had bought whiskey and cigars in Gibraltar, magazines and books, and I felt expansive. I was an international traveller. I knew the ways of the world. I told him. I told him what I did. 'I will come to visit you,' he said, smiling closer, revealing a gold tooth, and I realized at last that he was making overtures, that he was propositioning me, that his were the words of homosexual courtship. 'I'm sorry,' I said. 'That's not possible. I am going back to London tomorrow. I have a girlfriend there,' I said, and walked away, stood somewhere else on the deck, and I felt the danger, my foolishness and vulnerability, but how thrilling it was, too, to have this happen on the deck of a ship, with the brown hills of Africa running beside.

Tangier was full of danger of one sort or another – drugs, the police, robbery, violence; you heard stories all the time – but the greatest danger was something else. I perceived it and acknowledged it. I saw it in those Americans and Englishmen who had lived there for years, the painters, the writers, those who did nothing special or nothing at all but made themselves equally busy, the exiles, the expatriates, the foreign colony. Tangier was so easy. It was so uncomplicated. It was so cheap. It spoilt you for anywhere else. That was the greatest danger. It made you unfit for the rest of the world. Stay one day too long, you felt, and you were here for life.

I would miss it. I would miss the fatimas, the beggars, the jostling narrow streets, the smells, the dust, and the noise, the endless strangeness and the wonder of being in its midst. I would never forget it. I would leave. I would go to Paris and Finland and Berlin. Of course I would leave. But not yet. Not yet.

Orford asked a favour. His bank had made a mess-up somewhere. Nothing really, but a bother. Be sorted out in a week. Meanwhile, he said, he was a trifle stretched for funds. I took out my wallet. 'No, no, dear boy,' he said. 'I can manage. I'll get by. Very kind of you, though. No, no, what I wanted to ask you was something else.'

We sat in Benito's: the usual white wine, the usual *tapas*, the same scratchy tunes on the old record player. I hadn't seen Orford for a week. He looked terrible. His cheeks were drawn and grained with white stubble. His hands seemed to tremble even more than usual. His eyes were watery and pink.

'My friend in Spain is expecting me,' he said, 'and I'm afraid I can't get over right now. Got myself into a bit of a state, as you can see.' He smiled weakly. 'I wondered if you, if you're going across . . .'

'Well, I was thinking of going tomorrow,' I said.

'She lives in La Linea,' Orford said. 'You take the bus from Algeciras. Drops you right at the door. Very easy. You won't have any trouble finding it.'

'All right,' I said. 'Sure.'

'Oh, wonderful, wonderful,' Orford said. He seemed to brighten up at once. 'I'll write you a letter. Do it as soon as we get back. You can stay the night, which is what I always do. She'll give you dinner, too. She'll be delighted. Doesn't see enough people. Hardly sees anyone, actually. Lives with her mother, which is a bit of a problem. It's all a bit sad. A lovely woman. Russian. Very intelligent. Married an Englishman, just after the war.' Orford shook his head. 'Terrible mistake. Beastly fellow. Met him in Berlin. Well, you know, it was either that or go back to Russia, you know how it was in those days. Anyhow, he's dead.

Died two years ago. Can't say I'm sorry, either. A ruffian. Made Sophie's life hell.'

Orford reached for his glass. I put some money on the counter for two more.

'Very good of you,' Orford said. 'I'll write that letter at once.' He drank his wine and then he turned to me, his watery eyes full of apology. 'I'm putting you out, aren't I?' he said.

'Nonsense,' I said. 'Not at all. I like meeting new people. It'll be interesting.'

I stepped from the street through the front door into the sound of birds. It was late afternoon, five o'clock, after five. I was in a courtyard open to the sun. I had introduced myself. Now I handed over Orford's letter. Sophie put it in her pocket. 'I will read it later,' she said. 'Dear Orford. He telephoned me this morning. Is he all right? I know, I know, the drinking, always the drinking. Come, we will go upstairs. That is where I sit. We will talk there.'

A wooden staircase led up to the floor above. There was a balcony. I walked up behind Sophie. Birds darted past, swooping to the ground and up again, in and out of the open sky. They darted in black flashes, in endless flight. 'Oh, the swallows,' Sophie said. 'What a nuisance they are. It is impossible to be rid of them.' 'They're beautiful,' I said. 'Do you think so?' Sophie said, turning on the stairs to look at me.

Then a voice called out. 'Sophie?' I heard. 'Sophie?' We were almost at the balcony. 'Come,' Sophie said to me. She stood by an open doorway. 'Mother,' she said, 'this is a friend of Orford's. From Tangier. He has come to visit.'

She was tiny, like a ceramic doll, all pink and white. This was her bedroom. She lay on the bed in a dressing gown, propped up on pillows. Her bare feet were the smallest I had ever seen. They were perfect, like china. An open book lay face down on her lap. Her eyes were blue, like the sky above the courtyard. They seemed to hold all the life that she had. 'She speaks mostly Russian,' Sophie said to me. 'Do you speak Russian? No?' To her mother she said: 'Your supper will come soon. It is still early. I will come back then.' I smiled politely. The blue eyes smiled back.

I had brought a bottle of whiskey as a gift. 'Do you need ice?' Sophie said. 'Water is enough? My husband always drank with soda. The English way.' She made a face. 'Thank you,' she said, accepting a cigarette. 'Ah, this is pleasant.' We sat in a large room with windows onto the courtyard. There was a piano, a table set with chairs half hidden by a screen, dark paintings in heavy frames on the walls: landscapes, stern faces, glowing globes of fruit. Books lay about, magazines. There were flowers in vases, plants in pots. The light, despite the windows, was somehow European. The whole feeling of the room was European: cluttered, lived-in, lace, velvet, turned in on itself. Sophie crossed her legs, tilted up her chin to blow away smoke. 'Tell me,' she said. 'Tell me about the world.'

She was Orford's age, of Orford's generation, and in her face, under the age, there was that classical structure of character: the high cheekbones, the brow. But her eyes were otherwise. They were too quick, too nervous. There was something beseeching about them. They seemed to plead.

We talked. We talked, first, about Tangier, about Orford. Sophie sat forward on her seat, interested in everything I said, her eyes – those beseeching eyes – studying my face. She lit another cigarette. Then we heard her mother calling: 'Sophie? Sophie?' Sophie stood up at once. 'Take another drink,' she said. 'Please.'

This happened four times. The windows grew dark. The swallows fell silent at last. The paintings on the walls were like rectangular holes. I poured another whiskey. I could hear Sophie talking to her mother, footsteps, doors, hurrying sounds. I felt like an eavesdropper, alone in that European room. Then Sophie came back with an omelette, an opened bottle of wine. She pulled up a small table. We ate.

She wanted to know everything, where I had been, where I was going. She was interested in everything. It grew late. It was after midnight. Sophie didn't look in the least tired. If anything, she seemed more animated. She crossed and recrossed her legs. She lit yet another cigarette. She leaned forward. She perched on her seat, her eyes on mine, endlessly questioning. She wanted more. She would listen all night. I told her about the books I liked, the writers. 'Oh, books, books,' she said. 'What are books? I have books.' Her arm swept across the room. 'Books are not enough.'

She poured another glass of wine, the end of the bottle. She looked down. When she spoke again, her voice was one I had not heard before, a low voice, filled with bitterness. 'Oh, this Spain, this wretched Spain,' she said. 'How I hate it. How I long to go. But how? Where?'

I shook my head. 'It must be very difficult with an invalid mother,' I said.

'Invalid?' Sophie said. She spat out the word. 'She is not an invalid. She is worse than an invalid. You thought her nice? You thought her a pleasant old woman? She is a monster. She lies on that bed. She watches who comes into the house. She knows everything. There is nothing wrong with her. She is not ill. She can walk like you and I. There is nothing wrong with her legs.'

Sophie stared at me. Her eyes were like running water, except there were no tears. Her cheeks were dry.

'When I married that man she took to her bed,' she said. 'That was eighteen years ago. For eighteen years she has lain on my throat.'

She stood up. She flung an arm to the windows, to the black night. 'Those swallows,' she cried. 'Those foolish swallows have more freedom than I. I am buried here. I have no life.'

I slept downstairs, in her guest room. Everything had been thoughtfully prepared: an oil lamp, a chamber pot, an Agatha Christie paperback by the side of the bed. There was an ashtray, a jug of water. I woke early, woken by the swallows. The courtyard was alive with them, with their darting and swooping, their wings, their song. It was very early. There were no other sounds. I sat on the bed fully dressed and read. When I heard footsteps I went outside. Sophie was in the kitchen, in her dressing-gown. 'You didn't sleep?' she said.

She offered me breakfast, but I said no, I had better be going, I had a lot to do. I thanked her for her hospitality. I promised to give Orford her best regards. I didn't say goodbye to her mother. The bedroom door was closed.

I caught the bus to Algeciras. I found a place with a jukebox, shelves of cigarettes and spirits and wine displayed like fireworks. I sat down at the counter. I ordered orange juice, coffee, a toasted ham sandwich. It was a new place. Everything was chrome and glass and mirrors. Wherever I looked I saw my face.

LOSING THINGS

MARIANNE CAN'T FIND HER PURSE. 'OH, FOR God's sake,' Leo says. The morning, like so many, inside him starts to tip.

Yesterday it was the car keys.

'No, but I remember this time,' Marianne says. 'I remember exactly. I gave Silas money to buy some milk, and then he brought me back the change, and I put it in my purse, and I put the purse straight back in my bag. Here.' She turns to her handbag, on the chest of drawers, but doesn't touch it. 'I remember Vasco watching me put it in,' she says.

Marianne looks down at the dog.

Leo takes a deep breath. He goes through the handbag.

Then under it. Around it. Pulls open the top drawer, where things so often get swept in.

Marianne opens her mouth but Leo cuts her short.

'Look,' he says. 'Just go. Go. I'll look for it later. Come on, the kids will be late for school.'

'Good-bye, daddy,' Deborah says.

Leo brushes her aside.

'I'm sorry,' Marianne says.

Leo forces a smile. He wants to say something too, a joke, a kind word, but he doesn't.

He stands staring at the floor until he can't hear the car any more.

Leo is writing a television play. It was promised for two weeks ago. He works in a room in a house ten minutes walk away, down the road and then across a park. A table. A chair. His papers. A few books. It is a small room, and no matter how he moves the table, the light is never right. On bright days it gives him headaches. Now that Marianne is working he could give up the room and work at home, but he won't. He doesn't want to do that. He has explained it to Marianne a dozen times. He needs his own place. No one touches him there. No phonecalls. No distractions. He says 'Good morning' to his landlady, Mrs Warburton, who is eighty-six, to Mr Warburton, who is ninety, and then has a chat with Mrs Warburton around ten, when she brings him in the morning paper and a cup of tea. 'The *murders!*' Mrs Warburton says. 'Nothing but *murders!* I don't know what the world's coming to. Where is it all going to end?' Leo laughs. Mrs Warburton laughs too. 'Isn't it *awful?*' says Mrs Warburton. Leo flips through the paper, drinks his tea, and then works till twelve-thirty, one o'clock. In the afternoons he cleans up round the house, listens to music, reads. He takes the dog for a walk. When the children come home from school he makes them something to eat.

Leo stands in the living-room, looking out of the window at the empty suburban street.

Another day down the drain.

He makes a cup of instant coffee, takes it into the living-room, sits down on the settee.

He is trying not to smoke so much, trying to keep it to ten a day.

He lights a cigarette.

I should have got out of the house before anyone was up, he tells himself.

He used to do that, and every night he'd tell Marianne how wonderful it was, the park still covered in dew, how alive his brain felt that early in the morning.

'The birds!' he'd say. 'The air! How people can sleep in and miss all that, I don't know. I get my best ideas walking across the park first thing in the morning.'

When he'd first met Marianne, he'd worked only at night. Starting around midnight, going till three or four. 'I never work in the day,' he had told her. 'I just can't. It's impossible. It's not my time.'

Habits?

Excuses?

Leo is suddenly edgy, too impatient to sit. He drinks his coffee quickly, stubs out his half-smoked cigarette.

It'll be somewhere obvious. In the kitchen. In the bathroom. Staring you in the face.

Yesterday, it took him about two minutes to find the car keys. He sat down and thought, here on the settee, squeezed his mind to focus on the keys, on Marianne's movements, where she'd been, what she'd done, saw her firmly in his mind, and then he went straight to her dressing-gown and there they were, in the pocket.

It's not in the kitchen. Not in the bathroom. Not in the bedroom. Not on the table next to the telephone in the hall.

He takes the cushions off the settee, feels around the back. He lies on the floor to look underneath.

Vasco licks his face.

'Oh, go away,' Leo says.

Not in the dining-room.

Maybe it slipped behind the bookshelves.

Leo peers into a black tangle of cobwebs.

A woman comes in to clean once a week, three hours on Friday morning. Marianne found her somewhere, made the arrangements. Leo came home early one Friday and heard the cleaning lady having an argument with someone in the kitchen. 'I will not! I refuse! Absolutely not!' 'Is that so?' said another voice. 'Is that what you think?' 'Hello?' he said, loudly. Mrs Hessler was standing all alone in the middle of the kitchen, doing both voices, her cheeks bright, her hair wild.

Leo looks at his books grey with dust.

Before her there was a Greek woman who made the taps in the bathroom gleam. She must have spent the entire morning on them. Everything else was untouched. Marianne wrote her a note listing what she wanted done in the house. The next day the Greek woman phoned to say she couldn't clean any more, she was going back to Thessalonika. 'Good riddance,' Leo said to Marianne. 'I'm sorry,' Marianne said. 'I'll find someone else.' 'Ah, it doesn't matter,' Leo said, suddenly angry. 'Who cares?' And then walked out of the room quickly, red in the face.

Leo stands in the kitchen doorway looking at the break-fast dishes.

He feels his anger rising and quickly lights a cigarette.

It was the doctor's idea that Marianne should work.

'Best thing in the world,' he said to Leo. 'Get her out of the house. She'll meet people. Office life. Believe me, there's nothing like office life to get your mind off things.'

But Marianne hates her job.

She comes home so tired, worn out.

And three mornings a week there's the analyst.

She hates that, too.

Leo sees suddenly that morning, the empty pill bottle, the dried spittle, Marianne's lifeless face.

He squeezes his eyes tight, fleeing, wants his brain to be blank, wants –

His eyes spring open. He can see the purse! Of course! Why didn't he think of it before? It has been made up into the bed. He smiles, almost laughs out loud. He hurries to the bedroom, pulls back the bedcover, then the blankets, the sheets.

He can't believe it when it's not there.

Leo sees his life: a white porcelain plate slipped to the floor. And look, the pieces put together, mended, glued, nothing missing, invisibly done, but it's not the same, it will never be the same.

Leo is close to tears.

He can't stand like this. He hurries to Silas's bedroom.

Silas is ten. Last night Leo and Silas had played gin rummy together for the first time. 'You can't hold your cards like that,' Leo had said. 'Look at them. How can you see what you've got, for God's sake?' 'I think I've finished,' Silas said, putting his cards down awkwardly on the table. Leo had stared at them, speechless. 'Have I won?' Silas had said. 'Beginner's luck!' Leo had shouted, swooping them quickly up. 'Best out of three!'

Leo looks at Silas's clothes lying in a tangle on the floor, at his guitar, his yellow transistor radio, his collection of Star Wars cards pinned to the wall over his bed. Comic books. His Snoopy doll.

He slides open a drawer, looks at socks, handkerchiefs, gloves, a belt, doesn't touch anything, closes the drawer quickly.

Deborah's room.

In here he feels even worse.

Two months ago Deborah came home from school with a ten dollar note. 'I found it,' she said. 'Where?' Leo had asked. 'You can ask anyone,' Deborah had said, and then burst into tears and run to her room. She was still in her room when Marianne came home. Marianne went in to talk to her. Leo stood in the doorway. 'I can even show you where,' Deborah said. 'So why are you crying?' Leo said. 'It's all right,' Marianne said, wiping away Deborah's tears. 'I believe you. Come on,' she said to Leo. They sat on the settee. Leo lit a cigarette. 'It's me, isn't it?' Marianne said. 'It's because I'm not here.' 'Nonsense,' Leo said. 'All kids steal. You have to be firm with them, and then they stop. That's all they want. A bit of authority.' 'No,' Marianne said. 'It's me. I'm a rotten mother. I'm a rotten everything.' 'Ah, come on,' Leo had said. 'Stop it. What do you want from yourself? Look, she's going through a phase, that's all. All kids have them. Come on.' But Marianne wouldn't look at him. She sat looking down at her hands on her lap. Leo felt useless, and then anger rising. He had stood up. The next day Deborah had given Leo a drawing of a flower she had made at school. *To Dear Daddy*, she had written along the top. Down at the bottom she had drawn a hundred kisses.

Deborah is eight.

Leo stares at the crack in the wall near Deborah's bed that he has meant to fix for months. He looks down at his feet.

And then, looking up, he sees on Deborah's bookcase that photograph – a snapshot, really – of Marianne in Paris, Marianne aged eighteen, before he knew her, standing on the deck of a boat on the Seine wearing a captain's hat and laughing with her eyes and his heart lurches.

He feels suddenly swamped with love. He has to tell her. He has to talk to her.

In the hall he dials most of Marianne's office number but then something makes him hang up.

The purse.

That damn purse.

Leo sits again on the settee.

He searches every room in the house, not moving from the settee, seeing each place sharply in his head, every detail, every corner. He reconstructs the morning. Silas going for the milk. Silas coming back. Marianne in here, her handbag on the chest of drawers.

But I've looked in the drawer. All the drawers. And underneath.

He looks there again.

He stands, thinking.

The garage? The laundry?

But she didn't have time, he argues with himself. But maybe, when I was in the bathroom . . .

He sees Marianne running outside with the purse, pushing it away, somewhere deep, dark, running back to the kitchen, straightening her face.

His eyes feel suddenly hot.

'Oh, don't be silly,' he says out loud.

It's not in the suitcases in the back of the laundry.

It's not under the towels.

Leo stands hot-eyed in the garage.

He moves boxes, newspapers, the lawn mower, tools. Everywhere he touches, spiders run.

Not there.

Not there.

Not there.

The children come home from school. Leo makes them toasted raisin bread. He pours out glasses of orange juice.

'Are you sure you didn't take the purse up to the shop?'

Leo asks Silas. He doesn't wait for an answer. 'Look,' he says, 'just run up and see, O.K.?'

Deborah gives Leo a drawing of a rabbit. The rabbit is surrounded by kisses and little hearts.

She sits on his knee.

'Tell me a story,' she says. 'Tell me about the talking bow tie.'

Leo lifts her off.

'Come on,' he says. 'Not today. I'm not in the mood.'

Leo is drinking whiskey when Marianne comes home. Jazz booms on the stereo. He doesn't turn it down. Marianne sits down beside him. She touches his hair.

'I can't find it,' Leo says.

'Leo,' Marianne says.

'Are you sure you had it?' Leo says. 'You didn't leave it in the office? It's not in the car?'

Marianne puts her hand on his. Leo stands up and adjusts the stereo.

'I'm losing my marbles, aren't I?' Marianne says.

She wants to hold him, to be held by him, but his cigarette is burning in the ashtray.

'Nonsense,' Leo says, not looking at her. 'It'll turn up.'

Leo sits with a magazine. Marianne is in the bathroom. It is ten o'clock. The children are asleep. He flips the pages. Nothing interests him. He can't concentrate. He reaches for his cigarettes, and is suddenly aware that he can't hear anything. No sounds of water, of movement. Nothing. Silence. She has been in there a long time. Leo's heart begins to pound.

The bathroom door is closed. Leo can hardly breathe. He bites his lips, and then quickly opens the door. Marianne, in her dressing-gown, is standing before the mirror, taking off her make-up.

'Oh,' Leo says, 'I didn't know you –'

Marianne turns to him, smiling.

'It's all right,' she says. 'You can come in. I've nearly finished.'

Leo sees his face in the mirror and has to turn quickly away.

Morning.

Leo walks from room to room, around and around the house.

Ten o'clock.

Eleven.

Twelve.

He stands in the garden, his hands by his sides.

Look, he says, if you don't like your job, don't do it. We don't need the money. Just quit.

Marianne doesn't say anything.

Look, he says, I know you don't like the analysis, but what else is there? What else can we do? Tell me. Look, he says, do you think I enjoy it? Do you think I like having you come home tired every day, watching you all the time?

Leo in the garden stands baffled and impotent, unable to move, hot with tears.

The children come home from school.

'I still can't find that purse,' Leo says.

Deborah looks at him, and the next thing he knows, she is holding it in her hand.

'Where was it?' Leo says. 'Where did you find it?'

'It was in the drawer,' Deborah says. 'In there.'

Smiling, pleased, she points to the living-room.

'Deborah!' Silas shouts. 'It *wasn't* in the drawer! Daddy

79

looked in there!'

Leo spins from his daughter to his son.

'Be quite, Silas!' he snaps. 'How many times have I told you not to speak like that in the house?' And he raises his hand to strike him, and just as he does his eyes are scalded by that photograph of Marianne, Marianne on the boat on the Seine in Paris, Marianne aged eighteen, laughing with her eyes, before he knew her, before she knew him.

TELL ME WHAT YOU WANT

'BUT EXACTLY!' CRIED MY AUNT. 'CHAIM?
It's a miracle. I can't believe it. Look how he smiles. It's
Sam to the *inch*.'

My uncle sat in a corner, his hand to his chin. 'A little,'
he said. 'Perhaps.' He spoke slowly, quietly. 'Perhaps
there is something.'

'Something? What do you mean something? Would I
scream for a something? I opened the door and look what I
saw. It's Sam.'

She crossed her legs, tapped ash from her cigarette, sat
back, leaned forward again, an excitable woman, intense,
somewhere in her sixties, her firm eyes never once leaving

my face. Aunt Rivkeh. While my uncle sat in his corner, slowly stroking his chin.

'So,' she said. 'So.' She smiled. I smiled back. She recrossed her legs. And then, suddenly serious, leaning forward, 'But why didn't you come sooner?' She gave me no chance to reply. 'Tell me,' she said, looking straight into my eyes, 'have you eaten?'

I nodded, quickly. 'Please, don't worry,' I said. 'I had something in Tel Aviv.' My stomach growled. I tried to cover it by clearing my throat. I blushed. I reached quickly into my jacket for my cigarettes.

'So you're a smoker?' Aunt Rivkeh said. 'Here, an ashtray.' She was up, she was sitting again, one minute stern, the next smiling, but her eyes always the same. She watched me light my cigarette. 'So tell me,' she said, 'when did you arrive?'

'I got into Haifa this afternoon,' I said.

'Haifa? You came by ship? Straight from Australia?'

'Well, no . . . from Greece. Rhodes. I've been living there. Actually, I've been in Europe for nearly two years. I was in London . . .'

'Nearly two years!' She looked at me astounded. 'So why didn't you come here before?'

I had no answer. I looked down. 'I was working,' I said. 'In London.'

'London, London, what's London? If you want London, take a trip. This is your *home*!'

I didn't know what to say. I felt my skin prickling under my aunt's firm eyes.

'Well . . .' I said.

Silence sat heavy in the room. I had been judged and found guilty. I was shallow. I was a fool.

'Rivkeh,' my uncle said. 'Make some tea.'

'London,' Aunt Rivkeh said. She gave me a hard look – puzzled? annoyed? – clicked her tongue, took one more puff of her cigarette and crushed it out, and then quickly she went out of the room. I heard her in the kitchen, plates rattling, cupboards closing with a bang. I looked across at my uncle, silent in his corner.

Was he older than my father, younger? It was impossible to tell. He sat hidden behind horn-rimmed spectacles, a solid man, serious, and perhaps he was even smiling at me.

'Ah . . . you write books?' I said. My uncle gave an almost imperceptible nod. 'We used to get them,' I said. 'At home.'

Still my uncle said nothing, one heavy hand slowly kneading his chin.

'I'm afraid I didn't read them,' I said. 'I can't read Hebrew.' My uncle said nothing. His face stayed the same. 'Actually, dad didn't read them either,' I said. 'Not one of them. Never. I don't think he even looked inside.' Oh, fool, fool! I shouted to myself, what are you saying, why are you telling him these things? But I didn't stop. 'He used to read Westerns,' I said. 'Cowboys. Shooting.' My uncle blinked slowly behind his horn-rimmed spectacles. I didn't know what to say next. 'Ah . . . cigarette?' I said, leaping to my feet.

I looked desperately around the room.

'You have a nice place here,' I said.

My aunt saved me. She swept into the room with tea in glasses on a tray, plates heaped with cake. 'Here,' she said. My stomach growled mightily and again I covered it with a cough. I picked up a piece of cake.

'Nu!' said Aunt Rivkeh. She lit another cigarette. She smiled, watching me eat. 'Tell me about yourself. What do you do, how do you live? I want to hear everything.' She leaned forward, her smile dropped away, she looked deeply into my eyes. 'Tell me about Sam,' she said. 'Your father. How did he die?'

I gave my aunt an edited version of my father's death, an acceptable version. That he had had a brain haemorrhage. That he had been ten days in hospital. That the doctor's hadn't been able to do anything for him. That he had died.

'Are you listening, Chaim?' my aunt said. 'Are you listening?'

I came to an end. No one said anything. My aunt looked at me with her firm eyes. I looked down.

'He should never have left here,' my aunt said at last. 'It was crazy. Everyone told him not to go. We pleaded with him. No. He had to go. What is Australia? What is that? But tell me,' she said to me, 'Was he happy there? We wrote him letters. He never answered. Was he so unhappy?'

'I don't know,' I said. 'I don't think he was happy. He used to talk sometimes about coming back. He had a friend, Popov –'

'Popov!' my aunt cried. 'Don't talk to me about Popov! He came here, to us, for help, this Popov. He was looking for something. He wanted . . . but who knew what? Not Popov! So we found him a job. A nightwatchman. Well, it's not much, but what can you do with such a man? Even from this he was thrown out.'

'Popov was my father's friend,' I said. 'The only one.'

'You hear that, Chaim?' my aunt said. 'Popov was his only friend.'

My uncle raised his hands, he shrugged, but still he said nothing, still his face stayed the same.

'But what's the matter with me?' Aunt Rivkeh said, jumping up from her chair. 'I must phone Horowitz. I must tell him you are here.'

'Rivkeh,' my uncle said. 'The boy's tired. He's just arrived. Let the boy sit.'

'What are you talking about? How can I not phone Horowitz? Sam's son. They worked together,' she said to me. 'Practically like brothers. I'll be one minute. Take more cake.'

She was gone. I was alone with my uncle again. I heard her in the hall, dialling a number. My uncle stood up.

'Come,' he said. 'I will show you my books.'

He took me into a room filled with books, shelves from floor to ceiling on all four walls, tightly packed, not an inch of space to put another. On a table, on two chairs, more books stood in stacks.

'History,' my uncle said. 'All history.'

'And yours?' I asked.

He pointed to a shelf. I saw again the small red books we had had at home, but a longer line here, almost an entire shelf. 'Footnotes,' my uncle said. 'Digressions. Arguments, suggestions.' His face grew animated. 'But we'll talk more tomorrow. Come, your aunt is ready.' He slipped back behind his passive face.

'I have done it,' Aunt Rivkeh said. 'You will meet Horowitz in a minute. It is all arranged. Go outside, he'll be waiting. He lives just here, the next street. Go now. Chaim, can you believe it?' Aunt Rivkeh ruffled my hair, and then took a step back to look at me. 'It's Sam, it's Sam.'

I walked with Horowitz in the streets of Jerusalem. Sun shone from a blue sky. Horowitz pointed out buildings as we walked.

'That one,' he said. 'And that one, and that one. All built by your father. Sam and I cut the stones together. Look there.'

He pointed to a small park, three or four benches set on a patch of lawn, bushes, trees, the park in a little hollow you went down to by steps.

'That was the quarry,' Horowitz said. 'That's where we

cut out the stones. Now it's a garden. Come, I'll show you some more.'

Horowitz walked briskly, his feet hitting the ground hard, an old man not come to terms with his age. His hair was snow white, flowing back from his forehead in thick, full waves. His eyes were pouched, his face lined and creased, the folds at his throat pinched in by a tight collar. He didn't wear a tie. His trousers were baggy, patched, shiny in the seat. The elbows in his jacket had gone. He had about him still the air of a labourer, as he walked briskly along the street, striking the ground hard with his boots.

'Here,' he said. He stopped. Bearded chassidim in long black coats hurried past. I saw stalls and shops selling fruit, old clothes, copper pots, brass plates. Through an open doorway I saw Jews at prayer. The air smelt of spices, smoke, dung. People shouted. Children ran.

'This street where you are standing now,' said Horowitz, 'was built by your father. These very stones.' He knelt down, peering at the stones closely, as though he were reading a book. 'Yes,' he said. 'These are Sam's stones. You can still see the marks he made with his hammer. Come and look.'

I knelt by his side in the street.

'Feel!' cried Horowitz. He slapped the stones with the flat of his hand, an immense noise. 'Feel how strong! In two hundred years they will still be here.'

A woman paused to watch us kneeling in the street. 'Look!' Horowitz shouted at her. With one hand he grabbed at her sleeve, with the other he pointed at me. 'This boy's father built the street where you are walking!'

The woman shook her arm free. 'So?' she said. She walked away.

'So you don't walk in the mud, where you belong!' Horowitz shouted after her, and then he laughed. 'Come,' he said to me, 'we will go now to my house. Tonight you

will eat with me. It's not so far from here. But you are
tired. All right, we'll take a bus.'

I sat with my father's old friend in Horowitz's garden, in
the shade of pomegranates, lemons, plums. Bushes were
everywhere, rough and wild. From some, flowers sprang.
We sipped hot tea in glasses and smoked cigarettes, sitting
on striped canvas chairs, Horowitz with his labourer's
hands laced comfortably across his stomach, his long legs
spread out, a breeze in his white hair.

'It's a beautiful garden,' I said.

'I built it,' Horowitz said. 'Before me there was nothing.
You see these walls? The paths? It's all my work.'

'It's a good place,' I said, and, sipping my tea, I saw my
father in our garden at home. It was Sunday morning. He
was mowing the front lawn. I saw him rushing out of the
house. A shout. A curse. I heard the lawn mower clatter-
ing down the concrete drive. It was an old machine, a hand
mower, rusty and stiff. The blades stuck. The wheels
locked. The whole thing jammed up. My father kicked it,
cursing, breathing hard. Ah! Ah! The blades spun again.
He spat on his hands, rubbed them together, grabbed the
handle. Then he ran, a savage, from one end of the lawn to
the other, the blades a blur before him, the grass a shooting
fountain. The blades stuck again. He charged on. He made
scars, skids, deep welts in the lawn. He didn't care. He left
wild clumps. Whole sections he ignored. When he bumped into trees, they shook to the very top. He tore off his
sweater, his shirt. He threw them at the house. Where they
landed is where they stayed.

Now I heard the front door opening, saw my mother
rushing out. 'Sam!' she cried. 'Sam! Put on something! Put
on a shirt! Everyone can see you! The neighbours!' She ran
to pick up his fallen clothes. He breathed like a horse.

'Leave them!' he roared. 'Leave them! I don't give a bugger about the neighbours! I don't give a *fortz*! They can kiss my arse! Go away! Leave me alone! Can't you see I'm busy here, I'm working?'

'Tell me,' I said, 'why did my father leave here?'

Horowitz sniffed. He unlaced his fingers. He tugged slowly at the lobe of an ear.

'Well,' he said, 'we had hard years.' He sniffed again. He ran a hand through his thick hair. 'Mind you,' he said. 'Terrible years. And then the war. And then our war. The British. The Arabs. Well, who can say what would have been? If he had stayed, would it have been better for Sam? For you? Who knows such things? Come, we'll go inside now. The sun has gone. I have wine, I have whiskey. Tell me what you want.'

LETTER

My good friend,

I write in a cloud of handmade Havana, a fine French wine uncorked on my desk. The cigar is a Monte Cristo, the full corona, that decent length, the wine a '74 Chateau Margaux. I tell you these things, my good friend, I list them here, not to browbeat you, not to boast, I do not seek to impress you in that crass way. I am no braggart, no self-trumpeter. You know that of me. You know that at least. No, my purpose is otherwise. It is to indicate to you, my good friend, that I am at my ease, I am relaxed, I sit here entirely unhurried, perfectly calm.

But, my good friend, don't misunderstand. I am not

drunk. Not in the slightest! Not in the least! I have made myself neither muffled nor muddled, I am not blurred, not besotted, certainly not sozzled, I am not, God forbid, sloshed. In fact, the opposite! Quite the reverse! My brain is sharp. My thoughts are clear. They have never been so clear. They are as sharp and clear as pinged crystal, the crystal of, say, the wine glass I reach out and ring now with my finger – do you hear it? – or fuller, deeper, of the weighted decanter on the tallboy to my right, from which, incidentally, I shall take, when my business here is done, my nightcap, a dram of noble Glenfiddich, that blessed single malt.

We are a little way from that moment yet.

It is midnight. I sit in my study. No need to describe it, you know it well. Have we not sat here often enough, my dear fellow, talking, laughing, enjoying a private moment, a quiet drink, reflected together in the glassed bookcases, side by side in these comfortably creaking black leather chairs? You have it? You can see it? You can summon up the scene? This is important. Let's get it right, old chum. Let's get it exactly right. So you will need the sounds too, allow me to supply them, let me give you, first, the gold-nibbed march of my Mont Blanc across this stiff paper, the lip kiss of cigar inhalation, the soft puff out, and now the wine, ah, the silence, the breathing, the lovely liquid tumble as I refill my glass.

You have it?

You have it now?

It is, as I've said, midnight. The household is asleep. The dogs in the laundry, the cat in the kitchen, each in its proper place. The children too, Sebastian and Melanie, in their rooms upstairs, Sebastian's the first door off the landing to the left, Melanie's beside it, the second. Do you know those rooms, old pal? Looked in, ever? Been inside? Sebastian's with its fine boyish clutter, his kites and swords, Melanie's with its pink patterned wallpaper tidy and neat.

And to the right, the other way along the landing from the top of the stairs, is my bedroom. Where, on her side of the wide double bed, the left as you look in from the door, lies, gently sleeping, my wife.

Celia.

Sweet adorable Celia.

The strap of her silk chemise has slipped, in her sleep, from her left shoulder – she lies on her right – affording us uncluttered not only that palely glowing apricot but the beginnings of a breast, that softer, riper fruit. She is so gently asleep. See how her lashes softly fall, those gentle Japanese brushstrokes, how her hair lies, that tossed-back careless cloud of curls. Her lips are moistly parted, and seem to smile. You know that smile. So charming! So innocent! Beside her profile on the pillow, the tips of the fingers of her left hand shyly peep.

Do you have it? Can you see?

Come along, old bean. There is light enough. The room is far from dark. The drapes are ajar. The moon floods in.

Feast your eyes, old stick. Feast your eyes.

Oh, and the chemise. I should have mentioned. To give you the details, to get it exactly. The chemise is lavender. The palest silk lavender, like the faintest bruise.

You see it? You have it? You know it, the one I mean? Hmm, you bastard? Do you know that particular one?

Hmm, you scum?

Old chum, the game is over. It is finished. It is done. You have rutted with my wife for the last time. You have rutted with my wife enough.

Sweet adorable foolish Celia.

I know it. I know it all. The times, the days, the dates. I know it in its every sneaky detail, its every smallest despicable thing.

The jig, I'm afraid, old chum, is up.

So.

Good friend, dear fellow, old pal, old bean, old stick, old chum, if you expect now from me a lecture on duplicity and deceit, on broken trust, a friendship betrayed, I am afraid you are to be sorely disappointed. You will get no such from me. Time is fleeting, after all. Let us not waste it with hollow talk.

Instead, I offer this.

You will, of course, never come here again. Never. Not ever. Not in the day and not in the night. As I am sure you must understand. And that if you ever even attempted to set foot on these premises, I would instantly and with the greatest pleasure break your every foul bone.

As is only reasonable and fitting.

However, to descend for a moment to the trashy parlance of the day, that is the good news.

The other is that if I come upon you anywhere, anywhere at all, I shall similarly strike you with all my might. In any circumstance, in any gathering. Understand this well, my friend. You are nowhere safe.

In the presence even of the Queen of bloody England I shall sledgehammer your stinking heart.

Have I omitted anything? Is there anything I have neglected to say?

No, I don't think so, old chum.

Do you?

*

And in the morning, three doors from his office, the husband stepped into an establishment providing Secretarial Services, taking his letter carefully from his pigskin briefcase, and handed it to the girl by the duplicating machine. 'A hundred copies, if you will,' he said. 'I'll stand exactly here.'

REWARDS

EVETT QUIT SMOKING AND WANTED A
reward. Well, you know how it is. Two packs a day for
fifteen years down to flat nil just like that and there has to
be something, right? some wonderful thing in return. And
Evett knew it and needed it and wanted it and her name
was Rosalie.

Meanwhile, he paced.

He stood at the window.

He stared out into the night.

The lights of the city lay along the horizon, a band of
brightness across the bay, two hours drive if you didn't
dawdle except you had to be careful of the cops. A

fabulous view. Stirring. Inspiring.

Rosalie, Evett said.

He was in the country, Evett, the weekend retreat of his friend Bill the botanist currently on sabbatical in the U.K. leaving the house to Evett to mow the lawns and tend the trees and pace away the craziness of no cigarettes now, not a single cigarette, for six days, eleven hours and forty-two minutes.

I want Rosalie, Evett said.

Evett was a playwright. Wrote plays. Used to write plays, that is. For fifteen years wrote speedily and easily always with a cigarette burning close to hand, but in the middle of the most electric scene, in the middle of a speech, in the middle of a sentence even, sometimes even a word, if he chanced to look across and there were no cigarettes left in the pack then that was it, either he went straight out and bought some more, or, more likely the case, bang, that was the writing business done for the day.

No smoke.

No words.

Finito.

Camels, too.

The strongest.

He had always smoked Camels, right from the beginning, fifteen years of heavenly Camels, except for a brief flirtation with Gaulois for some now forgotten reason, and then that period in England, in London, when Camels weren't to be had for love or money and what he smoked then were Players in those sealed tins of fifty that opened with a whispered whoosh and to get them out you pulled a paper tab in the middle and the cigarettes rose up in their tin like an immaculate white cathedral.

I want Rosalie, Evett said. I want Rosalie to come here.

Rosalie was a student. Rosalie played flute. Rosalie had black hair in thick curls that fell to her shoulders and the first time she came to see Evett she wore a green dress that dipped in the front and underneath no bra.

I'm going to undo you, Evett said.

Rosalie had big eyes she knew how to open beautifully wide.

Don't worry, Evett said. When I've finished I'll put you all back.

He was a smoker then, Evett. He felt fine. Was playwright-in-residence at a top university where apart from a speech at the beginning and a farewell party at the end, his only duty was to open his door if anyone tapped. Which Rosalie did. Rosalie wearing no bra.

And Rosalie, being Rosalie, hadn't come to talk about playwriting. Wasn't in the slightest interested in plays. Didn't mention them once. No, what she wanted to know about was London, where you stayed and where you went and what you did. Rosalie was vaguely thinking of maybe going to London someday soon.

And Evett sat her down on one end of the settee he had in his office and he sat himself down on the other end and he talked. He talked and talked. The Kew Gardens are wonderful, he said. The famous cast-iron greenhouses in the middle of winter filled with heat. Go there, he said. And Richmond Park too, with the deer. And the galleries, he said. The Rembrandts in the National, the Bacons at the Tate. And the bookshops are good, or used to be. And this is where you buy clothes. And these are the places to eat. Evett talked and talked and Rosalie sat and sometimes her eyes flashed wide and sometimes she just smiled and when Evett had finished he stood up and Rosalie stood up too and Evett put his arms around her. It seemed the most natural thing.

You're marvellous, Rosalie said.

I'm going to undo you, Evett said.

And when Rosalie widened her beautiful eyes he said,

97

Don't worry. I'll put you all back.

And he unzipped her and first he only looked – he marvelled, he exulted – and then he gently kissed each breast and then he rezipped her back into her green dress.

Hey, you did too, Rosalie said.

At the door she gave him her big eyes again and then a wink and she was gone.

It was only then that Evett heard the roaring of his blood. He had never done anything like that before.

Evett was forty and married. His wife smoked mentholated cigarettes. Evett sat alone in his office. No one came. No one tapped. Evett slipped out the phone book. She was married, she had told him – his eyes had fallen to her ring. She had laughed. Bayford, she said. He's a drip. Yes, there she was, hiding behind the letter B. Bayford. Evett remembered a Bayford at school, a gaunt boy with spots.

He closed the book quickly, as though he were being watched.

A week later Evett's wife had business in another city. Evett drank coffee, whiskey, smoked and smoked before he could make the call.

My wife's away, he said quickly. Come for dinner.

She wore the same green dress but this time with long black boots which gave it a completely different look. Evett had said eight and that's when she came, exactly on time.

Evett broiled steaks, tossed a salad, floated peaches in a glass bowl of iced water, opened wine.

Hey, I'm really hungry too, Rosalie said.

She ate her salad with her fingers, carefully folding up the leaves. She had the smallest hands, the fingers impossibly slim. You don't mind, do you? she said. Evett shook his head. She was like a child, a scampish child. Evett was entranced.

He had planned to serve coffee, chocolates, a liqueur,

but he couldn't. He couldn't sit a minute longer. He couldn't stay away.

Come on, he said, taking her by the hand.

But at the bedroom door she stopped.

Are you sure? she said.

It was the statement of the double bed, its statement of established solidity.

Absolutely, Evett said.

But when he turned back the bedspread, it was only to his side that he invited her, his section of the marriage bed's width, it was only on his pillow that he allowed her thick black curls.

He made her breakfast in the morning. Sun poured in the windows. Evett watched her impossibly slim fingers breaking off a corner of her toast. But when he moved to embrace her again she said no, better not, let me get off to work, and Evett didn't press.

O.K., he said.

Evett's wife was a consultant town-planner and she never laughed in bed, and Rosalie's husband was a mutual funds rep and a drip, but they were marriages, they were married, leave it alone, leave it be, and Evett did, and this month became the next month and then three months after that, and then suddenly Evett gave up his Camels – just like that quit his beloved cigarettes – and straight away he went loopy out of his mind pacing at Bill the botanist's place in the country staring at the lights of the city two hours away across the bay and all he wanted was Rosalie.

Six days, twelve hours and twenty-four minutes.

But why not?

Because I'm married.

So?

Because you don't.

You just don't.

Evett saw his wife sitting in her armchair in her corner of

the living-room at home. She was busy with a report. She was always busy. She didn't look up. She reached for her cigarettes. She blew out smoke. Alone in the country Evett heard the hard click of his wife's dry lips.

Evett dialed the number, staring at the lights.

I'm in the country, he said. Would you like to come up?

Rosalie's reply was immediate.

You mean for a naughty day? she said.

Yes, Evett said. Yes.

He gave her directions. It was complicated. There was a turn just past a stand of pines and then another one by a water pump, it was easy to miss, but at ten o'clock in the morning, exactly when he'd said to come, Evett heard the sound of her tyres on the gravel in the drive and there she was.

Easy, she said, smiling in the sun.

She stood by her car dressed in jeans and sandals and a red tartan top and cradled in her arms she bore fruit and cheese and wine – pears and brie and a long green bottle of hock – offering them up shyly, as though the gift of her presence were not enough.

These are for you, she said.

She had also brought Alfie, her dog.

Come on, Evett said, thick with joy. Come inside.

And he began to unbutton her before the wide windows that faced the view – a summer haze over the city and the waters of the bay – tumbling her out of her tartan, unzipping her free of her jeans, but the dog leapt, Alfie her playful labrador, wouldn't leave them alone, leapt and bumped and wanted games, and Rosalie said, Wait a minute, I'll put him outside, and through the windows Evett saw her naked in the sun and she was a nymph, a goddess, as natural as the landscape, running with her dog dappled through the trees, and then she was inside again in his arms and on the divan by the wide windows filled with sun she was as natural as the landscape, a part of it, all rising hillocks and flowing meadows and between her eager legs that bosky wood, and Evett felt endless and inexhaustible and each time he drove Rosalie opened her eyes beautifully wide and caught her breath as though he had reached right to her heart, right to her very heart.

Evett flowed into Rosalie with guiltless joy.

Rosalie kissed his fingers, each one separately, and then the palm.

And then sat up suddenly, her eyes wide again.

Are you starving too? she said.

Let's have it in the garden, Evett said.

And after lunch – the brie, the pears, the cool bottle of wine – he wanted her again and led her back inside, back to the divan by the wide windows and the landscape view, and no, it wasn't slower this time, it was just the same, just as it had been before, Evett endless and inexhaustible and Rosalie wide-eyed each time catching her breath as though he were reaching her very heart.

They rested.

They showered.

They dressed.

It was late afternoon.

It was time to go.

They would drive back to the city in their separate cars – Evett was going too. He had paced enough, it was time to go home.

Evett locked the house.

Well, he said.

Rosalie stood by her car.

Well, Evett said again, and he moved to embrace her but her face said no.

He stopped.

You don't love me, do you? Rosalie said.

No, Evett said. He shook his head.

For a second she was troubled – it was almost a frown – and then she smiled.

That's O.K., she said. I don't love you either.

And stepping forward quickly with two fingers she lifted up Evett's chin and kissed him quickly in the hollow of his throat, that most tender place.

I had a nice time, she said.

And then she turned and in the same movement slipped into her car and was gone.

Evett backed out.

Rosalie's car was silver – a little silver Toyota – and Evett saw it flashing ahead of him as he drove, in this lane and then that lane, the flashing reward he had needed and wanted and earned, and watching it he knew, as surely as he had crushed out his last cigarette, that it was leading him home to his wife, his marriage, the grim work to be done there, the golden rewards beyond.

RUSSIAN BOXES

FORTUNES TURN. DOORS SLAM. WINDS TEAR the grey tarmac. The music is the scream of jets. Today, as they say, is the first day of the rest of your life. And here is Ackerman, the Australian playwright, running through London, shedding money like autumn leaves.

It's years since he's been here. Is it really seven? All of seven?

Ackerman, running, shakes his head. Wind buffets his body, gusty and freezing, laced with rain. Ackerman, running, is red-eyed, tired, more than tired, beyond tiredness. He has no time for tiredness. Look how he bulges. From Simpson's, from Jaegar's, from Liberty's, from

Hatchards, from Harrods, from Fortnum and Mason's, the names on his packages proclaim his progress. 'Oops, excuse me,' he mumbles, colliding. 'Sorry about that.' Rushing along Piccadilly, his hands too full to wipe the rain from his face.

A cashmere cardigan?

A silk scarf?

A matched set of green briar pipes?

This is the Burlington Arcade, where Ackerman runs now, nipped in to quit the wind and the rain, head swivelling left and right as he rushes along its length, eyes sharp, missing nothing, the windows of the select shops flickering like stations from a train, left, right, left again.

Suede gloves?

A travelling chess set?

A fisherman's jumper?

The rain he has just quit shines and runs on his black leather jacket, spots and splashes and damps his rumpled corduroy pants. Ackerman's travelling clothes. Worn from Sydney to San Francisco and then all around New York. Hardly out of them, day or night. Ackerman travels light. Neglected to pack a hairbrush, needs a shave, his face as rumpled as his clothes, but who is there to bear witness, who is there to chastise?

An enamelled cigarette case?

A black leather diary?

A military band of red–coated lead soldiers marching in line in an elegant box for his son?

Ackerman pauses, considers.

His son was born here, in London, his daughter too; but they remember nothing, know only Australia; are oblivious to their father's history here, those seven thin years.

In Maida Vale, that first bleak room.

And then in Putney, where the table lurched, the light so dim.

Primrose Hill.

Notting Hill Gate.

On Hampstead Heath, those daily solitary walks, round and round, a playwright looking for words.

All those old haunts.

I must have been mad, thought Ackerman in Australia, when he thought about them, and laughed, goodbye and good riddance, who needs all that?

Ackerman, the new Ackerman, strode the streets of New York, a playwright's convention, until suddenly, out of the blue – Why not? It's so close – jumped on a plane.

Winds on the grey tarmac, the scream of jets, here he is.

The old haunts.

To actually see them again.

But didn't, hasn't.

Instead, is buying.

Clothes.

Gifts.

Bag after bag.

Money like leaves.

His son is too old for lead soldiers, but what does that matter? Ackerman has them, another weight, another bag, is rushing again, past the windows, this side, that side, head swivelling, not missing a thing.

And suddenly he stops again.

Boxes.

What are those boxes?

They are in a window of mostly silver: silver paper-knives, silver picture frames, napkin rings, tiny scissors, a display of expensive elegance.

Small painted boxes.

Made in Russia, says the card. Handpainted.

This one with a field of wheat, that one a stormy sea, a third of onion–domed churches, a sky of stars.

Ackerman sees his wife's joy unwrapping the un-expected gift.

He is awkward opening the door, fingers clumsy with bags, bursts in, his mouth already open to speak, to order, to enquire the price. The salesman looks up. He is busy with someone, a woman, an elderly woman, a silver tray lies on the glass between them, and Ackerman sees on his face a look of – is it alarm?

But of course. The leather jacket. The red eyes. Acker-man's unshaven rain-running face.

Ackerman quickly smiles.

But too late, already the salesman has reached down, has pressed a button, a buzzer, on the edge of the counter.

Summoning at once a second man, a burly man, out in an instant from a tight door behind a steep flight of stairs.

'Yes?' he says, a steely professional.

Oh God, thinks Ackerman, sagging in his bags.

For the button has summoned more than this man.

I know this place, Ackerman realizes, sinking. I have been here before.

*

'I've never liked it,' his wife said.

Ackerman stood with lowered eyes.

'Honestly. Look, have I ever worn it? Have you ever known me to put it on?'

'I know,' said Ackerman. 'But . . .'

'Come on,' she said, reaching for his hand. 'Please. Honestly.'

It was gold, in a blue velvet box that closed with a pin. A bracelet. His wife's gold bracelet. Given by a rich aunt when his wife had turned twenty-one.

'How much do you want?' the man asked him. This was in the first place, in Regent Street.

'Sixty pounds,' Ackerman said.

In the second place the man looked at Ackerman harder than at the bracelet.

'Fifty-five?' Ackerman said.

Ackerman walked the streets of London.

'Fifty?' Ackerman said.

Shop after shop, it was always the same. They volunteered nothing. You asked. They said no. Unless what you asked was what they would pay. Or – and this was the game – lower.

By the fifth place Ackerman knew what he would get. He knew it exactly. To the penny. But still he went on.

Another shop, another.

Each one a further humiliation, but impossible to stop.

'Excuse me,' said Ackerman, 'I have a gold bracelet I would like to sell.'

Regent Street.

Bond Street.

Piccadilly.

The Burlington Arcade.

(Where Ackerman stands now, hiding his unmasked face in the field of wheat, the storm at sea.)

'Ah, the hell with it,' says Ackerman, raining money down onto the pointless gifts. 'I'll take the lot.'

KICKING ON

SO LET'S HAVE LUNCH, SAYS CHARLIE, AND I
said fine. I mean, why not? Charlie is an old pal. We go
way back. Hell, we were at school together, for God's
sake. Oh sure, he is also a conman, a liar and a cheat, but
how often do I get to see the crazy bastard, how often is he
in town? Charlie lives in Hong Kong, London, Kuala
Lumpur too, I heard. He travels. He gets around. So I said
fine, O.K., when did you have in mind?

Tomorrow, Charlie says.

This is over the phone, this conversation. Sunday night,
eleven o'clock. I was practically in bed.

Tomorrow? Charlie, I said, tomorrow is Monday. No

one eats lunch on Monday.

Jesus, Nathan, he says. It has to be tomorrow. Tomorrow's all I've got. Nine o'clock Tuesday morning I've got a three million dollar appointment in Brazil!

How can you reply to that?

O.K., Charlie, tomorrow it is.

And bring Rupert, he says.

Rupert is a close mutual friend.

Fine.

So then I told Charlie where we'd go, this great new place I'd lately discovered, plants, mirrors, classy French wines. Listen, Charlie, I told him, this place is so sophisticated, it'll be a miracle if they even let you in. Ha ha, he says, not laughing. One o'clock, I told him, don't be late. I'll be there! he snaps, and hangs up with a crash like he's just dropped twenty plates, the most incredible sound.

So here it is Monday and I'm striding to the restaurant wearing what passes for elegance these days in my faded wardrobe, to wit, the only slightly frayed pale blue Brooks Bros shirt, my least baggy cords, plus the big hopscotch check tweed jacket I grabbed up in a sale in England a dozen years back and which still looks great if you don't try to do it up in the front, a splash of bright red hankie poking out of the show pocket to give it that extra bounce, and at one o'clock on the dot I push open the door and what's the first thing to greet the eye but not only Charlie already there, not only firmly ensconced at the very best table right in the middle of the room, but *eating*, the bastard, already eating, look at him, hunched over a monster plate of sausages, cramming them in like he's just jetted in from a famine.

I don't know why I don't just walk straight out.

But I don't.

I stand there.

I thought we were having lunch, Charlie, I say.

Charlie looks up.

Charlie is wearing these huge round glasses over his little peering eyes and with his little mouth hanging open like a beak for a moment he looks like a startled owl.

But only for a moment.

Shut up, he snaps. Sit down.

And back he dives to his sausages, cramming them in even faster than before.

I don't move.

What's the matter with you? Charlie says. Sit down.

I still don't move.

For God's sake! Charlie explodes, practically shouting now. This is breakfast! I didn't have breakfast. We'll have lunch in a minute. Now will you sit down?

I take a deep breath, in and out.

Charlie, I say.

But I can't be angry with him. How can you be angry with Charlie Hope? I mean, who else has ever phoned me up at three o'clock in the morning from Saudi Arabia just to say hello? It was unbelievable. I staggered out of bed and there he was, booming in my ear. Hiya, Nath! he shouted. How's tricks? Where are you, Charlie? I said. Where are you phoning from? It was somewhere long-distance, I knew, I could hear that rushing hollowness, that strange ethereal other-side-of-the-world clinking you get. Saudi Arabia! Charlie boomed. Jesus, I don't know, the capital, whatever it's called! I was speechless. I was flabbergasted. I didn't know what to say. Standing there in the dark, clutching the receiver, all I could think of was the technology involved, the science, the silver satellite flung into black space over our spinning planet just so Charlie's crazy voice could bounce off it at three o'clock in the morning and into my ear. It was lunacy. It was madness. I think I was close to tears. Except this was Charlie, of course, so it was a con, this was just the softening-up call, because the next morning he phoned again, he wanted me to send him books, magazines, a letter, who knows what exactly, he was trying to impress the pants off some zillionaire sheik, and so maybe I should have been disillusioned, but I wasn't. Not in the slightest. I was thrilled. A phonecall at three o'clock in the morning from Saudi Arabia just to con a pal! What class! What style!

I sit down.

Good, says Charlie. Listen, try some of this sausage, it's fantastic.

I wave it away. I haven't come here for a bit of sausage on a fork.

Charlie, I say. You look gorgeous.

Charlie's little eyes behind the huge owl glasses narrow at once, instantly suspicious. What? he says.

No, I mean it, I say. I really do. And I push back my chair, to get a better look.

He has blossomed a bit since I saw him last – well, who hasn't? – except with Charlie, never a slim fellow, what he looks like now is he's attempting to smuggle a watermelon past Customs under his shirt. What a belly! But what a great shirt too, a dozen colours at least in dazzling rainbow stripes. Really fantastic. I am truly envious.

Great shirt, Charlie, I say. Great shirt.

Charlie ignores me, back on his sausages.

Great tie too, I say, and it is.

In fact, Charlie all over is wonderful. A classic yachting blazer, cut like a dream. The softest grey flannel slacks.

And I'm just leaning forward to have a feel with my fingers when what do I spy under the table but sneakers! White sneakers!

Charlie! I say. All this and sneakers?

They're not sneakers! Charlie snaps. They're Gucci! Listen, Nathan, if I told ya *half* of what they cost, you'd have a heart attack on the spot!

I am, of course, suitably silenced.

Now up dances Sally, the owner of the place. Sally is tall and blonde and wonderful, with the longest slimmest legs she can scissor round my throat any old time. She used to be a top fashion model until she married Clyde and they started this. Clyde is a weed and works in the kitchen. Why do the gorgeous ones always marry weeds?

Everything all right, gentlemen? she says, splashing wine freely into our glasses.

The glasses here, I should tell you, are these huge numbers the size of vases where you can chuck in an entire bottle if you're not too careful.

Perfect, says Charlie. Lovely sausages. And he gives Sally a little pat on the bum.

Sally glows.

He's amazing with women, Charlie, really amazing. I don't know how he does it. I mean, if I tried stuff like that, I'd probably get thrown right across the room, except I wouldn't even dare do it in the first place.

Beautiful, says Charlie. Just what I needed, and I see his hand has gone from little pat to practically deep fondle. I have to look away.

Ha ha, laughs Sally, disengaging, but not really wanting to. Well, if you need anything else.

We'll wait for our friend, I say.

Where is Rupert? Charlie says. Did you phone him?

Come on, Charlie, I say. You know Rupert. Rupert is a baby. Rupert likes to come late. It makes him feel special.

Well, up him, says Charlie. Let's order.

I laugh.

Relax, Charlie, I say, relax. You've just had ten sausages. You can't be hungry. What's the big rush?

Charlie rumbles something I don't catch but I get the general drift and then lunges over and seizes a poppyseed roll.

He's incredible, Charlie. You wouldn't believe it, looking at him now, but he used to be a rower, this was at school, a runty fella but the most powerful pair of shoulders you've ever seen. He ran too, long distance, I think it was. Amazing. And look at him now. And what exactly is he doing in London, or Kuala Lumpur, or wherever the hell he is? Is he going to tell me?

So far, not a word.

So here we are, waiting for Rupert, with Charlie working his way steadily through the rolls and every five minutes Sally dancing up again and splashing more wine in our glasses and asking is everything all right gentlemen and the last time she danced up Charlie, I swear it, had his hand practically up her dress.

I thought she was going to come in her pants.

Jesus, it's one forty-seven.

And ah, hooray, at last, here comes Rupert.

Afternoon, boys, he says, sitting straight down with not the slightest apology for his appalling late-coming.

Well, let's face it, Rupert is a slug. Oh sure, he's genial, jovial, a great guy to have around and all the rest of it, but a slug nevertheless. You want some work from him? It'll be two months late. You want to have lunch? Make sure you've had a good breakfast before. That's Rupert, take it or leave it, that's how he is.

A quick lunch, boys, he says, arranging his napkin on his copious lap. I shouldn't even be here. Got a lot of work to do.

Big deal, says Charlie. Right, let's order. I'm starving.

He's already had ten sausages, I tell Rupert.

Shut your face, Nathan, says Charlie. Anyhow, it was only six.

I give Rupert a wink. Rupert, I should tell you, comes in various sizes, depending on which diet he's into at the moment, and today, I see, he's down to just two chins and

114

only a medium-sized mountain under his snazzy loose-fitting casual velour top. Very elegant, the Rupert, when he tries.

O.K., let's eat, I say.

So we wave over Sally and after endless discussion all settle on pasta for starters followed by pepper steaks, and I don't know what we talk about over lunch, the usual dirty jokes and stuff like that, mostly, the usual lewd remarks and outrageously ribald suggestions about every passing female we happen to spot, certainly nothing serious, nothing about work or anything personal or what's doing in Kuala Lumpur or London or wherever the hell Charlie is, and we laugh a lot and Sally keeps splashing in that wine and finally the bill comes and I tell you, it looks like a phone number.

Jesus, we all gasp.

Except, well, we've had an enormous amount of wine, of course, all those endless bottles Sally kept splashing into our glasses, plus the obligatory brandies and ports at the end with our cigars, it all adds up.

But who cares, what a great lunch.

We somehow stand up.

Darling, says Charlie to Sally, giving her right tit a huge maul, that was wonderful.

Any time, gentlemen, she says, her face flushed as all hell, either because of the fortune she's just made out of us, or because of what Charlie is now doing to other various parts of her gorgeous body.

But finally we're outside.

God, it's after four o'clock.

Listen, you bastards, says Rupert, I don't know about you but I'm going home. I've got an enormous amount of work to do.

Me too, I say.

But no one moves. We just stand there.

And then Charlie sees this amazing thing.

The restaurant, I should tell you, is in this little street, a sort of cul-de-sac, nice and quiet but with office windows all around it looking down, and there on the footpath, in amongst the bags of garbage waiting to be collected, is a toilet. I mean, someone is chucking out a perfect toilet, the whole thing, complete with lid, and before we know what's happening, Charlie has lifted up the seat, taken out his old boy – a hideous sight in itself – and is having himself an unhurried piss.

I mean, this is in broad daylight.

This is in the middle of the street.

This is with four hundred windows staring straight at him full of outraged secretaries half of whom are already phoning the police.

Christ, Charlie! I say. What are you doing?

Very considerate, says Charlie, pissing grandly, the person who put this here. Very thoughtful.

You're a swine, Charlie, says Rupert. You're a beast. Come on, he says to me, let's get out of here.

You mean, just leave him? I say.

Absolutely, says Rupert. Come on.

Wait, wait! cries Charlie. I haven't finished!

Too late, Charlie, too late, because we're off, Rupert and I, charging up the street, Charlie in mid-piss wearing his best owlish expression and the outraged secretaries now banging on their windows in total disgust.

We puff up the street, Rupert and I, round the corner, then collapse in a doorway, both panting like mad.

Crazy bastard, says Rupert. Serves him right.

Still, I say. We shouldn't have left him like that.

Why? says Rupert. Did he tell us what he's doing in Kuala Lumpur? Not a word, the secretive bugger. Come on.

We puff on.

Where are you parked? I ask Rupert.

Next street, he says. Listen, what about a glass of champagne for the road, freshen up the palate after all that wine?

Well, I say.

Come on, says Rupert. Just one glass each. I can't have more, I've got work to do.

So the next minute we're in this dim and elegant bar and Rupert is ordering a half-bottle – a split – and then we're raising our glasses.

To Charlie, Rupert proposes. Long may he piss in the street!

And we've hardly wiped our lips when who should walk in but Rodney Potter, Rupert's top drinking companion when he's not having lunch with me.

Uh-oh, I think.

Boys, says Rodney. What a pleasant surprise.

Potter is a stubby fellow with a balding pate and a fine drinker's paunch and what he does for a living exactly I've never been able to find out but whatever it is it certainly doesn't consume too much of his time. One of the great drinkers, Potter.

Hey, do you come into bars all by yourself, Potter? I ask him. I couldn't do that.

Naah, he says. I saw Rupe's car round the corner where he always parks it when he wants me to come and have a drink. It's his signal.

Uh-oh, I think, and if ever there was a clear signal to me to go home, this is it, but I don't.

What's all this half-bottle rubbish? says Potter, advancing to the bar behind his stomach. What are ya, old ladies or something?

I think we should get Charlie back, says Rupert. I'm going to phone the bugger and tell him to come back in.

Charlie who? says Potter.

And I don't know if it's the second or third bottle we're

on when Charlie comes in, looking sheepish and outraged both at the same time, if you can imagine such a thing, behind his huge owlish glasses.

Shut up, Charlie, says Rupert by way of greeting, before Charlie can even say a word.

I better phone the missus, I think, tell her where I am.

Hell, it's seven o'clock.

I'd better go home.

Potter is in the middle of some raucously complicated story about a chap who had a domestic tiff and to make a subtle point sawed all the furniture in half.

Did that include the toilet seat? Rupert asks, giving Charlie a wide elbow nudge.

Charming, says Charlie. Very charming.

God, it's eight o'clock, I've got to get home.

Listen, says Charlie, are we gonna eat or anything? I'm starving.

Good idea, says Potter. I know this great place. We'll get a cab.

And we do, but the great place is closed, this being Monday night, and so are the next two great places we try, and by now Charlie is really starving and Potter is dying of thirst and Rupert has run out of cigarettes and what we'd better do is repair to some nice quiet bar somewhere where we can plan our course of action over a glass of refreshing ale.

The nice quiet bar has a sign on the door: No sneakers.

These are not sneakers! Charlie roars at the bartender. These are the best Italian hand-made Gucci!

We won't be long, says Potter. Look, there's a sofa. Sit on that.

Serves him right, says Rupert, waving his arm for a bottle of champagne.

So Potter and Rupert and I plan our course of action over a couple of bottle of champers (Must phone the missus! Must go home!) leaving Charlie to cool his sneakered heels outside, and when we've got it all sorted out, out we go again, and what do we find but Charlie deep in conversation with a gorgeous number similarly banned because of the sneakers on her pretty little feet.

Leslie, says Charlie, giving us all a big wink. Meet the gang.

We pile into a cab.

Much laughter.

Watch it, Les, says Charlie. Ya just got me with your left tit right in the eye.

Ha ha, laughs Rupert. Stop complaining.

Where we're going is either the Hilton or the Sheraton, anyhow, somewhere big that's bound to be open on a Monday night so we can sit down properly and have something to eat, and I don't know where it is we finally lob but the story is the same. Closed. No food. Nothing.

Well, what about a drink at least? says Potter.

I'm sorry, says the fellow we're talking to at the desk. You have to be a guest.

Well, bugger it, says Rupert, slapping down his credit card. O.K. Let's have a room.

We pile into the lift.

Much laughter.

Hey, this is great, says Leslie, opening up the mini-bar fridge.

Charlie meanwhile is on the phone ordering up hamburgers and ice cream.

My watch says it's either one or two o'clock. Whatever, much too late to disturb the missus.

Fabulous view, says Leslie, sliding open the glass doors onto the balcony.

Fantastic, says Charlie, close behind, one hand already rummaging in the general area of Leslie's bum.

What a scrubber, says Rupert.

119

Cheers, says Potter.

The hamburgers arrive, the ice cream.

Rupert signs the bill. It's only money, he says.

Grub's up, I announce.

We're gonna need some more champagne in a minute, Potter says.

Leave something for us, you bastards, Charlie calls from the balcony. He and Leslie are a dark shape out there in the night it's better not to see.

We eat.

We drink.

It's three o'clock in the morning.

Where's Rupert?

I am not asleep, he says, opening one eye on the toilet. How dare you accuse me of such a dastardly thing.

I've got to go home, I think. I've definitely got to go home.

I come out from the bathroom and there is Charlie on the bed, pants down, his and hers, Charlie and Leslie hard at work. For the second time I glimpse his old boy, that hideous sight.

Potter is on the balcony, alone with a bottle of scotch.

I'm going home, I tell him.

What's the rush? he says.

The cab driver behind the wheel outside wakes when I open the door.

Where to? he says, and lights a cigarette.

The park across the street is unreal in the night, not a single leaf moving, as still as a dream.

We drive through empty streets, neither saying a word.

I'm home.

In bed my wife is drawn over to her side as she so often is, and when I move to put my arms around her, for comfort, for warmth, for solace, for love, she draws herself even more firmly away, excluding me, her legs bunched tight, her arms, her curved back as hard as a shell, curved away from me, curved firmly away.

Jesus, I say, or think I say, and I don't know if what I feel is guilt or bitterness but what's the difference, it doesn't matter, I close my eyes and a minute later I'm asleep.

Rupert phones the next night, his voice fine and shouty, the same old Rupe.

Hey, that Charlie, he booms. What a rat. The way he got into that scrubber.

I stand in the hallway with the phone to my ear and the mirror on the wall beside me showing me my face. Lines. Shadows. Tired eyes. I don't look good. I don't look good at all.

What happened? I ask. What time did everyone leave?

I don't know, says Rupert. I think I had a little kip in the bathroom. Anyhow, when I came out everyone was gone. Even Potter, and he never leaves till the end. So, well, inasmuch as I was paying for it all – an absolute fortune, by the way – I figured, what the hell, may as well use the room properly, so I got into bed and had a decent sleep. Rupert laughs his boomy laugh. Very nice too, he says, if you avoided the wet patch over on one side.

Ha ha, I say, staring at my face.

I don't know what time I got out of there, Rupert says. Must have been about eight. Eight, eight-thirty. Somewhere round there. I got a cab. Actually, I was amazed, he says. I felt fine. Amazing recovery. Never felt better. And then I come in the door here and here's everyone eating bacon and eggs and straight away I have to race into the bathroom and chuck.

Rupert's laugh clubs my ear.

There's something about bacon, he says. I've always found it nasty after you've had a good night.

ARCHITECTURE

SUNDAY EVENING, NINE O'CLOCK, THEO stands bent over his drawing board set up on the dining-room table, the table glass-topped, an embroidered doily beneath, the board on a sloping stack of old *Esquire* magazines, a far from perfect arrangement – the magazines slither, the board drifts and tilts – the work before him a hotel in the mountains, golf and tennis, horseriding and restaurants, pools, spas, luxury suites, eighty miles from the city, a steep site overlooking a lake. For ten o'clock Monday morning, a scant and rapidly slipping thirteen hours from now, Theo has to provide plans, elevations, parking facilities, diagrammatic traffic flow, other details, a full-colour rendering of the whole scheme too, five sheets of work at least, an impossible amount, if he works right through the night it probably still won't all get done, the project set two weeks ago but Theo only just started, Theo labouring now on the basic floor plan, the very first sheet.

'What's the time?' his father says.

Theo, drafting, halts midline.

'Nine o'clock,' he says. 'Just on.'

'They said they'd phone.'

'Dad,' Theo says. 'It's only been an hour.'

Theo catches something in his voice and has to look quickly down.

Theo's father is in the front room, directly in front of him, through the open connecting double doors. The doors are sand-blasted glass, a stylized stag left and right leaping a rainbow and billowing white clouds. His father sits in an armchair angled to a far corner, so that Theo's view of his father – a lumpy, puffy man – is of grey grizzled hair, the back of his head, the flushed stuffed roll of the back of his father's neck, but a side slice of face too, an ear, a round cheek with its ash of bristles, the ponderous creases and folds of the lid of his father's left eye. This is when Theo looks up. But even when he doesn't, when he is bent over his drawing board, sketching, scribbling, calculating, drafting, working it out, getting it done, he can still see him, his sloping shoulder, his arm, his left hand lying on the armrest of his chair, an unmoving heaviness of flesh printed on the edge of his vision, impossible to dislodge.

'You don't think we should call them?'

The ink in Theo's full pen quivers.

'Dad,' he says.

They ate early, were finished by six. Theo's father made the meal. Then Theo set up his drawing board on the dining-room table and his father sat in the armchair in the front room. This is where Theo's father always sits, his armchair, his place. The armchair is placed to face the television set in the far left-hand corner of the room. Theo's father loves television. He watches it every night. He switches it on the minute he comes home from the factory where he works, a loomtuner in a woollen mill, something less than a mechanic, servicing the machines. He loves police things, detectives, gangsters, anything with action and fighting and shooting, but his real favourites are westerns. These he truly adores. 'The cowboys,' he calls them, tilting up his chin. He puffs. He beams. He fills the house with runaway stagecoaches, high-noon shoot-outs, the strident voices of steely men herding cattle, blasting lives. He thumps the armrests of his chair with his fists, urging them on. 'Shoot! Shoot!' he cries, his round face glowing, an exuberant sun. He is transported, in another world. Theo's father was a pioneer in Palestine as a young man, laid the telegraph line from Haifa to Tel Aviv, worked in a quarry in Jerusalem, 'A real life,' as he endlessly tells Theo, 'but what would you know?' Twice this evening Theo's father has pushed himself heavily up, lumbered across to the television, clicked it on. At once sirens, gunshots, roaring music filled the house. Theo's father stood, bent at the set. Then both times, both times it was the same, he grunted, sighed, growled, muttered some sour word, clicked it suddenly off, lumbered back to his chair.

'Ahhh,' Theo's father breathes.

'What?' says Theo, looking quickly up.

For the twentieth time the magazines slither, the drawing board crookedly slews.

They went to see her this afternoon, at visiting time, three o'clock. Theo's aunts were there, uncles, family friends, others too, people Theo barely recognized, a crowd around the bed. Theo stood where he could. He saw his mother's eyes encircled with black, her white face, her apologetic smile, as though this were all her fault, how sorry she was to be causing such a fuss. She spoke to this person, that. Voices babbled around the bed. Theo stood. Then someone pushed in front of him, pushed him aside, as though he were still a child, disregarding him completely, pushed him away.

Theo feels a hotness, a tightness flying to his eyes.

'I'm making some coffee,' he says. 'Would you like anything?'

His father silently sits.

Theo hurries out of the room.

In the kitchen Theo puts a light under the kettle, quickly gets out the coffee, the milk. A cup and saucer. A spoon.

God, he thinks, looking at the sink.

They had fried eggs and salami for dinner. Slices of cucumber. A cut-up tomato. Theo's father is no cook, thick-fingered in the kitchen, clumsy, a splasher, a breaker, a spiller, and this meal was no exception, the egg yolks broken, the whites burnt, everything greasy with old oil. They sat in their usual places at the kitchen table, his father at the head, Theo to his right, the table to Theo strange, lopsided, out of balance, as it has been ever since his mother was taken to hospital, these past two weeks. Her empty chair was like a hole. Theo couldn't look there. He ate with his eyes down. There was no conversation. The meal was quickly over. Then Theo stood up. 'I'll clean up,' he said, but his father was too fast for him. 'Leave it!' he snapped, sweeping everything into the sink, the dishes, the frying pan, drumming cold water on top. Their eyes caught for an instant. Theo looked quickly away. 'Ah, what's the difference?' his father growled. 'So they'll soak.'

Theo feels again that hotness, that slap to his eyes.

The kettle whistles.

Theo carries carefully his coffee into the dining-room.

'Are you sure you won't have anything?' he asks his father. 'The kettle's just boiled.'

His father says nothing.

Theo sips his coffee, as quietly as he can.

Theo's initial image of the hotel was a floating curve that fitted into the mountains, weightless and flowing, a wall of glass alive with light, reflecting the wide lake. He picks up a pencil. He looks at his work on the drawing board. For a moment he feels hopeless. Come on, he tells himself. It's only a project. It'll do.

'Is it ten o'clock yet?' his father says.

Theo looks up to see his father's head rising from the armrest. He is rubbing his face, the eyes first, squeezing, then down, the nose, the bristled cheeks – their rub like a roar in the silent house – his lips, his chin, then his hand falling away, lifeless, heavy, falling back onto the armrest of his chair.

'I'll phone them,' Theo says. 'Do you want me to phone them?'

His voice is too high.

His father doesn't reply.

Floor plan. Main services. Front elevation. Side. Theo unpins the sheet, pins down a fresh one. He straightens the magazines. He moves his T-square into place. He stretches for a moment, draws back his shoulder blades, rotates his head, eases his cramped back. He looks down. The new sheet seems to him already soiled, spoilt, an exhausted surface before he has even begun.

'Eleven o'clock,' his father says. 'It must be eleven o'clock.'

Bent over the blank sheet, Theo thinks of the first design project he ever did, a kindergarten for blind children, a year and a half ago, his first project in his first college year.

He remembers how he ran across to the library, spent the entire afternoon there, reading everything he could find. What blind children needed. How they felt. Surfaces. Sounds. Textures. Warmth. The ways they perceived the world. He scribbled notes, page after page. And then, hurrying home, in his room, on his table in the corner, his small desk, with papers and pages and wide-open books spread everywhere over his bed, and music playing – he always had music going when he worked, gorgeously clumpy Dave Brubeck on the record player thumping out the blues, the needle lifted each time it got to the end and put straight back on again – his brain ablaze with grass and pebbles and tanbark paths, and chimes too, and bells, and each child's locker with a different shape in its door, a square, a circle, a five-pointed star, in two joyous hours Theo had danced out his design. But not before Theo's father had appeared, home from the factory, looming in Theo's door. 'Ssh,' Theo's mother had said. 'He's working. For school.' 'Working?' his father said, a quick look over Theo's shoulder, bumping, dismissive, his usual mocking tone. 'You call that working?'

Theo sees his face reflected in the glass, mirrored above the table's dark wood. Beneath the glass the imprisoned doily patterns his forehead and cheeks.

'Come here,' his father says. 'Sit here.'

It is midnight. The house is silent. The hospital hasn't rung. Theo sits with his father, the room's other armchair pulled across, side by side in the front room. Theo, like his father, looks straight ahead. His father sighs, an engine of breathing. And then Theo feels his father reaching across and taking his hand, where it lies on the armrest of his chair.

'We mustn't lose her,' Theo's father says. 'We mustn't lose her.'

Theo is embarrassed. There is something wrong. It is

not his father's voice. It is a forced voice, phony and unnatural, like his father's foolish westerns. It is not true. Theo feels his father grip his fingers but he doesn't squeeze back. He sits. He looks straight ahead. He wants this moment to be over. He has to get back to work. He wants his father to let go his hand.

THE NIGHT WE ATE
THE SPARROW

IT WAS WORSE. WHEN I WOKE UP THAT morning for a moment there was nothing – I was normal, perfect, it had never happened – and then I must have moved or something because suddenly there it was, just as before, that steady painful throbbing. And I didn't need to touch it to know, or to look in a mirror. No, it wasn't going to just go away. It was bigger. It was worse. Somehow I got up, somehow I got dressed, somehow I made myself some sort of breakfast – thin instant coffee on my impossibly slow hotplate, brittle biscuits, crumbly cheese – and then I put on my boxy acrylic fake fur overcoat and went down to the Finchley Road to look for a doctor. I was

131

twenty-eight years old, an Australian in London in the Swinging Sixties, Carnaby Street, the Beatles, dolly birds, the centre of the world, new excitements every day. The week before I had seen John Lennon climbing into his famous black-windowed Mini, in the middle of Soho, as plain as day. And this week, out of nowhere, I had been struck down by a Biblical affliction, the lowest of the low.

A boil.

A boil on the backside.

A boil on the bum.

It was the day before Christmas. Finchley Road was busy and bustling, people all over the place. Everyone was hurrying, laden with purchases, in and out of the hectic shops. Nobody looked at anyone else. It was very cold. A wind like icy water blew straight into your eyes. On the footpath outside the tube station fir trees were being sold, men shouting, women grabbing. There was barely room to get past. I could just see myself getting bumped. I could already feel the pain. I took a breath, waited for an opening, and then scuttled through like a crab, elbows out, heart pounding. Made it! I found a chemist's, went in and asked could they tell me where the nearest doctor was – a routine enough enquiry, you would have thought, but I stood there fiercely embarrassed, as awkward and un-comfortable as a spotty adolescent buying his first con-doms. My eyes, I knew, were red and wet from the killing wind. My boil throbbed madly as falsely I smiled.

It was a five-minute walk, up one of the side streets off the Finchley Road, to the left, a narrow red-brick Vic-torian semi-detached behind a beaten hedge. The waiting room was the long front room of the house. It had a grand piano in it, with a vase of flowers on top and a photograph of an earnest little girl standing with her dog. The little girl was wearing a Brownie uniform and smiling very ser-iously at the camera. The piano and the flowers and the little girl in her Brownie uniform standing with her dog made me feel somehow guilty and belittled, as though I had intruded on a private life. Twenty hard chairs lined the two opposite long walls, facing each other across the room like armies. I didn't sit down. There were about six people ahead of me. The room smelled of furniture polish and cold. Someone coughed. I dropped my eyes at once. When it was finally my turn – there was no one after me, no one else had come in – I hurried in to the surgery, quickly unbuttoning my coat as I went, that foolish fake fur.

He was standing when I came in, one of those colourless balding middle-aged men wearing a vaguely shabby dark-blue striped suit. I was aware at once of thin lips, long, cold, feely fingers. 'Yes?' he said. He looked annoyed even before I spoke. I started to tell him what was wrong, my hands going to my belt. 'Piles, is it?' he said, his eyes shooting straight into mine, his thin lips twisting up into an unmistakable sneer. 'No,' I said quickly. 'It's nothing like that.' I undid my trousers. I heard him grunt behind me as he stooped, fish-cold fingers touching me sharply, then away. When I straightened up he was already at the basin in the corner, scrupulously scrubbing. 'It will burst,' he said. 'Buy some cotton wool. Clean up the mess.' That was all. That was the entire visit. That was all he said. He tore open the door for me to leave. I barely had time to rebuckle and zip. But that wasn't the end of it. I was just going out of his front gate when he pushed past, wearing a black overcoat, pulling on leather gloves. He didn't look at me. He ignored me completely. It was as though he had never seen me before, as though I didn't even exist.

I bought some cotton wool. They were doing it on special at Boot's, a huge display just inside the door. This must have seemed to me like some kind of omen and I over-reacted wildly, toiling back up the Finchley Road with more than enough to stuff a pillow. Alone in my room, I wasted no time. I turned on the light, pulled the curtains, hurried out of my coat and trousers. Then, positioning myself before the gloomy full-length mirror on the door of the massive inky-black wardrobe that bulged out into my cramped and crowded shoebox of a room – my tiny room with its bed, its table and chair, the long bookcase, the overstuffed armchair, the wardrobe and cupboard and hotplate, my suitcase and trunk – crouched down, corkscrewed around, my neck practically dislocated trying to peer over my right shoulder, I attempted to make a serious assessment of the situation, to evaluate exactly the state of affairs.

Yes. There it was. I stared and stared. To tell the truth, it didn't look all that terrible – a swelling, a redness – but what did I know about boils? I had never had one before, not ever, not once. No one in the family had ever had one either, that I could remember, not the most far-flung relative, the most distant cousin. A neighbour? Someone at school? Nothing. No one. Boils had played no part whatsoever in my life. Up till this past week, that is. Up till now. I bent. I craned. I peered. I stared. It throbbed. And then I began to have doubts. I saw the doctor's distasteful sneer, the thin lips, the malicious eyes. What if it wasn't a boil? What if it was something else? I saw, suddenly, emergency ambulances, plasma bottles, tubes and clamps. Hideous surgery. Hours under the knife. At the very least, I would never sit properly again. Jesus, I said, swept with self-pity. And then I saw myself in this obscene crouch in front of this mirror in this gloomy shoebox of a room, this room where I worked, ate, slept, read, thought, brooded, entertained, made love, and it was all too much. It was humiliating. It was demeaning. An enormous depression began to settle over me, wave after wave, an endless, leaden rain.

I stood slowly up. And God, look at the time. It was

way after four. I had done nothing, no work at all, not a scrap. I hadn't even had lunch. The entire day flown with this cursed boil.

My stomach rumbled. I began to think about making some coffee. And then I remembered – I had to be at Baker Street at five. I was meeting Kate there. There wasn't time for coffee. There wasn't time for anything. I grabbed my coat and was out the door, running. Or what passed for running in my present condition.

I got there on the dot of five, panting from my charge up the escalator in the tube, and of course she was late, but that was fine, it gave me time to recover. And then she appeared wearing a very tailored pillar-box-red suit with a short skirt showing off her wonderful legs and her eyes smiling and her hair swinging and I kissed her and we walked around the corner and slipped into a pub.

'How's the boil?' she said.

We were at the far end of the bar, away from everyone else, that part where they made sandwiches. There was a ham on the bone on a white serving stand, some impossibly red tomatoes. Streamers and holly decorated the mirror behind, a touch of Christmas tat. Katherine sat perched on a stool, I stood awkwardly propped against mine, not quite standing, not exactly sitting either. Katherine took out her cigarettes – her blue Gitanes – and I lit one for her. The boil throbbed grandly.

'Is it all right if I have a gin and tonic?' she said. Her eyes danced. 'I always get excited at Christmas.'

'Sure,' I said. 'Whatever you like.' I waved the man behind the bar over, ordered Katherine's drink, and a half of bitter for myself.

'Merry Christmas,' Katherine said, clinking glasses, and when I didn't look suitably exuberant, 'Oh, come on,' she said, 'boils are nothing. I used to get them all the time when I had my pony.'

'I went to a doctor this morning,' I said.

'Oh?'

For a moment she looked alarmed, her eyes serious, searching mine. And then they flicked with impatience.

'Well, go on,' she said. 'What did he say?'

'Cotton wool,' I said. 'He told me to buy some cotton wool.'

'Exactly!' she said. 'I told you boils weren't serious.' The concern fled from her eyes. They smiled again. 'Come on,' she said. 'Drink up. I've got to be at my grannie's at six. You can walk me there.'

It was just around the corner, a staid block of portered flats, old-fashioned, very proper. You could feel the hush the moment you stepped inside. There was no one in the lobby, no one watching, no one passing through, but when I attempted to put my arms around her, Katherine ducked away. She frowned. She shook her head. 'Not here,' she said, and kissed me quickly on the cheek. 'See you on Boxing Day. Give us a call from the station, I'll come and pick you up.' For a moment the concern flicked back into her eyes. 'And stop worrying about that boil!' Another quick kiss on the cheek, and then she was gone, whisked away from me up the heavily-carpeted silent stairs.

She was having dinner there, with her grannie, and then going into the country to stay with her mother over Christmas, a thing she did every year. Katherine's parents were divorced. I had been invited up for Boxing Day. I had not yet met Katherine's mother and felt vaguely nervous. I didn't know what Katherine had told her about me, about us.

We had been lovers for less than a month, tall, elegant Katherine and I. Although the first time I had seen her was almost a year ago, when she had danced in to the foyer at the publishers who had just accepted my first novel, danced in to take me upstairs for my appointment with their chief editor, her boss. 'I loved your book,' she said. Her eyes smiled. They were so direct. I was dazed. I didn't know what to say. I had to look away. I think I even blushed. We rode up in the lift together, this marvellous girl and me, and then the editor had talked to me about this and this and this, a fumbly man with terrible teeth, but all I was really aware of was that marvellous girl sitting so cooly at her distant desk, smoking a tipped Gitane. And then I had gone to Tangier, stayed there six months, lived in this room, that room, wrote, didn't write, stared into space, made plans, brooded, felt joyous, despaired, high times and low, good days and bad, and then London again, more rooms, the same, high times and low, good days and bad . . . and all that time – until finally I had phoned her, summoned up my courage, said let's have a drink – all that time I had kept somewhere tucked away in my mind that tall, elegant girl with the smiling eyes and swinging hair who had danced in to the foyer at the publishers and said to me so directly, I loved your book.

I took the tube back to Hampstead but I didn't go back to my room. I couldn't. I couldn't face it. The prospect of sitting there all alone in that furniture-jammed gloom, boil throbbing, mountain of cotton wool at the ready, was too depressing. It was just impossible. Instead, I bought some chocolate from a machine at the station and then I walked down the hill to see a friend.

Actually, there were two of them, Percival and Graham, fellow Australians sharing a bedsitter, a ground-floor front room always noisy with traffic, wide windows facing the busy road. Graham was a trainee editor at the BBC, bored to pieces on some current affairs programme, desperate to get into films. He was a rushy fellow, zooming with impatience, on permanent buzz. He edited like a whirlwind, a glass of red wine by one hand, a cup of black coffee by the other, an endless stream of cigarettes flying to his lips. He could work twenty hours at a stretch. He didn't need sleep. He knew what he was about. When he wasn't working he was bored. Percival was the opposite, tall and ungainly, nervous and unsure. He was studying drama at RADA. He had won a scholarship for which there had been over four hundred applicants from all over the world. This had only made him even more nervous. I don't know what sort of actor he was, but he was a wonderful mimic. He could do anyone. A superb James Mason. A flawless Laurence Olivier. A total Fred Mac-Murray right down to shoulder movements, eyebrows and cheeks. I finished my chocolate and knocked on their door. 'Yes!' someone shouted. 'Come in, for God's sake!'

The room was in its usual crazy disorder, its usual loopy mess. The TV was on, a radio was blaring, the Beatles were spinning and shouting on the record player just inside the door. '*Paperback wriiiterrr!*' they wailed. The beds were unmade, clothes were thrown about, wet towels hung limply from the backs of chairs. Everywhere you looked, on the beds, on the floor, on the chairs, on every conceivable surface, were newspapers, scattered, flung open, flung apart. It was as though a gale had just blown through. In that corner of the room that served as kitchen, a narrow cluttered benchtop separating it from the beds, Graham was frying sausages and boiling peas, a pall of steam and smoke billowing out. And in the centre of it all, arms sinuously aloft, eyes dreamily closed, face turned up rapturously to the smoggy ceiling, oblivious to everything save the music of the Beatles, danced endlessly long-legged minuscule mini-skirted Nelly, Graham's recently acquired hairdresser girl.

'Percival's not here,' Graham said, barely looking up. He was too busy. In fact, he was positively frantic. He darted and ducked, eyes narrowed, sausages spitting, gulping the inevitable glass of red wine, sucking on the inevitable cigarette. 'You had dinner? What about coffee? Sit down, it'll be ready in a minute, we're going out.'

'Hi,' I said to Nelly.

A lashed and mascaraed expressionless eye opened then closed, the gyrating pelvis not missing a beat.

I looked at the TV. The sound was off. A shouty face was flapping its mouth all over the screen. Then another face came on, this one against a brick wall, the hair blowing. How crazy it was, all that passion and commitment, when you couldn't hear a word. And boring. I bent down and picked up some newspaper. Then I bent down and picked up some more. It was really everywhere.

'Will you stop tidying up, for God's sake!' Graham shouted. 'We like it just the way it is. Leave it alone. Sit down.'

I cleared a chair and sat down. This was now extremely difficult for me. The best I could do was a kind of slumped sideways slouch, a skewered-around sitting on the hip.

Graham came from the kitchen part into the room proper somehow juggling his cigarette and his glass of wine and two plates of food. He put one plate down on a chair. 'Coffee's coming,' he said. He took one last quick deep drag then stubbed out his cigarette in a saucer on the floor. 'Come on, Nelly!'

He was already eating, before he had even sat down, fingers grabbing at the hot sausages, the peas too, mouth blowing, too impatient for cutlery, gulping wine. I tried not to stare. He really was incredible, the fastest eater I'd ever seen.

'Where are you going?' I asked him.

'East End,' he said, shovelling in sausage. 'This amazing new place. Great music. Top bands. They've got these fantastic dancing girls in a cage. Mick Jagger goes there all the time. We'll have to hurry.'

He finished what was on his plate, drained his wine glass, crossed his legs, lit a fresh cigarette. He really was incredible, in ceaseless motion every second of the time. Now, exhaling, he looked at me properly for the first time.

'Hey, what are you sitting like that for?' he said.

'I've got this boil,' I said.

He was still chewing but now he stopped. He stared at me. His whole face stopped.

'On the bum?' he said. 'A boil on the bum?'

He couldn't believe it. His eyes popped. His mouth fell open. He couldn't believe his luck.

'Nelly!' he shouted. 'Did you hear that? Look at the way he's sitting! He's got a boil on the bum!'

I thought they would be sick laughing.

'All right, all right,' I got in, finally. 'It's not that funny.'

The kettle whistled. Graham, still laughing, jumped up.

'Come on,' he said, handing out the mugs. 'We're leaving in exactly one minute.'

'Me?' I said. 'I'm not coming. God, I can hardly walk, never mind standing around in some ridiculous crowded dance.'

'Shut up,' Graham snapped, gulping his coffee. 'Of course you're coming. Stop being such a black cloud. I know you. You'll love it when you get there. You're always the same.'

We went in Graham's Volkswagen, me in the back. The boil by now was in constant throb and every slightest bump murder, Graham totally ignoring my pleas to for God's sake slow down, Nelly twisted around in her seat laughing insanely each time I rose crying out with pain into the air.

I must have been totally mad to agree to come.

'Nearly there!' Graham shouted. 'Hang onto your boil!'·

Nelly of course cackled at that too.

The place was dreadful. It was worse than dreadful. It was exactly the nightmare I had most feared, a dark crush of jam-packed jostling bodies, senselessly surging and stomping and elbowing. There was practically nowhere safe even to stand.

'I can't see Mick Jagger,' Graham said, eyes shooting in every direction, puffing on yet another cigarette.

Nelly, unbidden, threw herself into her usual gyrating.

I stood where I could, up against a wall.

The boil was really throbbing now, even when I stood perfectly still. Now I could feel it all the time, a heavy pounding presence, impossible to ignore.

Graham raced away somewhere and then he was back. 'Come on, why aren't ya dancing?' he said. 'There's birds here galore.'

'Listen, I think I have to go home,' I said.

'Rubbish,' Graham said, darting away. 'We haven't even seen Mick Jagger yet.'

I stood. I smoked. The crowd surged and elbowed. The music screamed. It was interminable. We would never leave. When I lit a match to look at my watch it had somehow got to be eleven o'clock.

'Graham,' I said, the next time he darted up. 'I really can't stand here any more. I really can't. I can hardly even stand up.'

'But what about Mick Jagger?' Graham said.

'Graham,' I said, 'I think I have to go to a hospital.'

It must have been the word that did it, or maybe there was something in my face. Graham shot me a quick look, and then just as quickly away.

'But what about Mick Jagger?' he said, but his heart wasn't in it. 'All right,' he said. 'Wait here. I'll get Nelly.'

Any kind of sitting down was now quite out of the question, a completely impossible thing. I crouched in the Volkswagen on all fours, throbbing boil aloft, a whimpering back-seat dog.

'A camera!' Graham shouted. 'If only I had a camera!'

Nelly's mascara ran with tears.

We drove back to Hampstead, there was a hospital there.

And yes we found it and there was a light on in Casualty and it was all going to be all right except coming out backwards out of the Volkswagen I somehow slammed myself against some stupid poking-out part of the door-jamb, a hinge or something, unleashing at once such an indescribable shock of pain all I could do was hysterically laugh.

I roared like a lunatic, a red-faced madman.

Graham, for his part, turned instantly white.

And that's how we were, a crimson maniac, a white-faced ghost – with a smudged-eyed doll awkwardly to one side – when the Pakistani nurse or clerk or attendant or whatever he was burst out of his office and demanded to know what was going on here, who was sick, why had we come at such an ungodly hour, was this a joke?

'It's him, it's him!' I pointed at Graham, turning him an even more horrified white.

A nurse cleaned me up, bandaged me, dressed the wound. The Pakistani was still furious. He fumed and glared. 'Why did you not come here earlier,' he bore down on me, helpless on the table, 'with such a condition as this? Are you such a madman absolutely?'

He filled out a card. I was to come back the day after Boxing Day. A doctor had to examine me properly.

'Ten o'clock in the morning,' he read out the card. 'Don't be late. It is in your interest, after all.'

So then it was Christmas Day and then it was Boxing Day and then it was ten o'clock in the morning on the day after. The doctor was a woman, very stern, about fifty. She was crisp and brisk. I lay, she looked, then she told me to get off the table, get dressed, sit down.

It was not a boil. It was not an ordinary boil. It was an operation. It was surgery. It was the knife. What I had was a pilonidal sinus, she told me. An impacted hair. Sometimes known as Greek's Disease, she said. The Greeks being a hairy people, she explained. She smiled coldly. Also called Jeepdriver's Disease. Another cold smile. I would be in hospital for ten days. Any questions? I didn't hesitate. My voice leapt out like an arrow. 'What if I just ignore it?' I asked. 'What if I don't have it done?' 'Then the poison in your system will work its way to your heart and you will die,' she said. Her smile this time was like a slammed door. I nodded dumbly, my eyes falling like my arrow useless at her feet. She began to flick crisply and briskly through a large black leather-bound book to see when next she was free to deal with my behind.

And the name of the hospital in Hampstead where all this happened? Why, the New End, of course. How could it have been otherwise? How could it have been anything else?

O Swinging London, O miraculous days, everything an adventure, everything brand-new. We shopped for pyjamas, Katherine and I, the curve of Regent Street still hung with its Christmas decorations, trumpets and angels, holly and reindeer, Bethlehem lights, though now what they celebrated was otherwise, the January Sales, all London's big stores solid with plundering hordes. I never wore pyjamas in real life, always slept naked, free between the sheets, but this wasn't real life, this was an adventure, the proper costume required, and somewhere between Jaegar's and Aquascutum we found the very thing, a deep royal blue slashed with scarlet on the collar and the pocket over the heart, oh very elegant, very suave, and when they told me at the New End the following afternoon to get ready for bed, I slipped them proudly on. Then off again, the bottom half, that is, while a male nurse shaved me. The tea trolley came round, but no, not for me, thank you, I'm not allowed anything, having my op tomorrow morning. Dinner the same. I sat up in my bed feeling splendidly well in my classy crisp pyjamas smiling at passing people – nurses, doctors, fellow patients – and read *Chicken Inspector No. 23*, S. J. Perelman's not-yet-out latest book – we shared the same publisher – a gift from Katherine. It seemed to take me hours to get to sleep – empty stomach, unfamiliar bed – but when finally I did I slept soundly, untrammeled by thoughts or dreams, and woke to a pre-med jab and then that magic childlike ride to the theatre, all ceilings and lights and faces smiling down. I was in safe hands. I was being looked after. I was warm. I was calm. I was completely relaxed. It was all a wonderful adventure. From which I woke vilely retching, reeking of anaesthetic, stenched and foul. And then the real pain, when I moved, when I tried to move, the flames and knives.

If Katherine came to see me that night, if anyone did, I was not aware.

But let me describe it to you, this wonderful hospital, or anyway that part of it that included me. It was not new. It was far from new. It was Victorian. The high ceilings were blotched with age, an atlas of ancient stains. The walls ran lumpy with pipes, high-knobbed antique switches, tides of long-ago encrusted paint. The floors were rattling bare boards. And the wards were public and long. We lay, my fellow patients and I, in two inward facing rows, twelve beds side by side, an identical long ward through the

doorway to the right. To the left were, somewhere, bath-
rooms, kitchens, administration, the outside world.

But the outside world, just then, was hardly my concern. I had been told to go in a bottle in the bed. 'Can't I
stand up?' I asked the sister. I had been trying for an hour. I
was close to panic. 'I can't do it like this,' I tried to explain.

'Of course you can!' she snapped. 'Stop being silly!'

When she was safely gone I struggled up, pulled the
curtain around, shakily stood.

'What's this for?' she cried, returned in a flash, ripping
the curtain angrily back.

Too late, sister, too late.

Katherine came that night, kissed me gently, held my
hand, asked was there anything special I needed, anything
I wanted at all. 'What about cigars?' she said, trying to
cheer me up. I shook my head. I lay. She sat. The visiting
hour fled.

The endless night stretched.

Around me, my fellow patients snored, moaned,
mumbled, coughed, awoke startled from their dreams,
stared upwards at nothing, lost in the night. In the morning, able to sit up slightly now, to move a little in the bed, I
began to sort them out.

In the bed to my right was a young black who had been
stabbed in the stomach, knifed in a fight. He lay there
stunned, made old in a second, grey with pain. 'And how
are we this morning?' the ward matron asked him, sweeping past. 'Better?' 'Yes, ma'm,' he said quickly, looking
terrified.

On my other side was a little man with a cherry-red face.
He was starving. He had adhesions, something wrong
with him inside. He couldn't eat. He wanted to but he
couldn't. I watched the nurse snatch away his untouched
breakfast, as she had snatched away his dinner the night
before.

'Still not eating?' she said, clicking her tongue. 'Naughty boy!'

'He needs help,' I said. 'I think he's starving.'

But she had already spun away.

Directly opposite, across the aisle, an old man lay dying of cancer, wasting away, his head already so insubstantial as to hardly dent the pillow. I stared at his sunken cheeks, the dry open hole of his mouth. They should have drawn the curtains around. I tried not to look.

Then there was an appendix, a hernia, a perforated ulcer, an operation for kidney stones. But the cast of characters changed rapidly, in and out, come and gone. No bed stood empty for long.

Percival came to see me on the third day. I welcomed him perched high on my bed on an inflated black rubber inner tube, feeling foolish and wobbly. Percival reacted at once. 'A *teeooob?*' he warbled, springing into his Edith Evans' Lady Bracknell in *The Importance of Being Earnest*. His fingers fluttered. His nose rose in the air. '*A rubbah teeeooooob?*'

Graham darted in with Nelly. Me sitting up on a rubber tube was just what he wanted to see.

'Hey, let's let the air out!' he shouted, making a mock attack.

Nelly brayed like a hyena.

'Be quiet!' snapped the ward sister. 'Where do you think you are? I'll have you all thrown out!'

My editor came, tongue-tied and toothy, bearing books.

My old Australian friend Charlie Hope charged in waving a pineapple. Charlie was in advertising. 'If I told ya what that cost,' he bellowed, throwing the pineapple onto the bed, 'you'd have a heart attack!' He banged me on the shoulder, couldn't think what to say, stood suddenly awkward in his immaculately flashy clothes. 'Jesus!' he cried, shooting a look at his watch. 'Gotta go! Look after yourself!' He stared hard at the pineapple and was gone.

And Katherine came. She came every day. I counted the minutes. The visiting hour each evening was at six, the staff as usual grumpy, no one allowed in a second before. But finally they nodded, and the doors were flung open, and in danced Katherine, eyes laughing, hair swinging, cheeks gorgeously flushed from the cold outside.

'I've brought you something,' she said.

It was a small package, elegantly wrapped. Fortnum and Mason, it said. A quail in aspic, a tiny naked bird in a jar. Ten and sixpence, it still said on the lid.

'For the man who has nothing?' Katherine said, raising her eyebrows.

'Pull the curtain,' I said. 'I want to give you a hug.'

She did, but it was no use. A sister whipped it back at once.

'This is not the Dorchester!' she snapped, glaring at us.

I lived for visitors. Visitors were something to wait for, to give you hope. They pulled you through the day. There was nothing else. The food at the New End was appalling – grey meat under gravy, some boiled-to-death vegetable, a runny pudding at the end. At breakfast the tea barely tasted, the porridge was like a watery paper-hanger's paste. And the servings were skimpy, minimal. There were no seconds. The food trolley rattled on the bare boards and was gone. It was Dickensian. It was all over in a flash. I was hungry all the time. Everyone was. But at least there were visitors, there were visitors to look forward to, there was that magic moment at six when they finally opened the doors, there was Katherine, there was always Katherine, flushed and smiling, dancing in.

But how quickly that hour fled. The ward sister rang a bell. 'Time!' she shouted. 'Seven o'clock!' Katherine left, everyone left, everyone was driven out. She would be back tomorrow, they would all be back, all my visitors and friends, but the thought refused to cheer me. In fact, the opposite. Now was not tomorrow. I stared into empty space, abandoned and bereft.

I couldn't sleep. It was way after midnight, almost one o'clock. I was wide awake. I was hungry. Dinner had been the usual skerrick of bloodless meat, the usual clump of watery cabbage, the usual runny custard with its thin dollop of jam. And all that anyhow more than five hours ago. Sleep was completely out of the question. I was just too hungry. I was starving to death.

I slipped out of bed. I didn't bother with a dressing gown or slippers. I didn't need them. I wasn't going far, only to the toilet, through the doors to the left, at the end of the ward. Except when I got there I kept going, quickly down a deserted corridor, and in a room that must have been some sort of servery – tea trolleys stood there, trays in stacks – I found in a cupboard a stale piece of cake on a plate. I ate it in the dark, hunched and wolfing, and then fled back to my room, heart beating with shame.

And did anyone notice? Did anyone ever find out? But who would have? And who, in that place, would have cared?

A nurse came to change my dressing in the morning. She stripped off the old, jammed a huge wad of cotton wool between my legs. 'Back in a sec,' she said, looking over her shoulder. 'Just hold it like that.' I held it like that for two hours before I acknowledged she would never come back.

They brought in a Pole, a Pole with a broken neck.

This was in the evening, after visiting time, my ninth night at the New End. I watched him being put into the bed directly opposite, just across the aisle, the bed where the old man with cancer had finally died. The Pole lay flat on his back, his neck in a harness from which two weights hung down over the end of the bed, a gaunt man, I saw, long and bony, with thinning hair and a white moustache.

'What happened to him?' I asked a sister.

'Drunk,' she sneered.

He had been in a fight. He had fallen down a flight of stairs. He was still unconscious. The weights and harness were to keep his neck in traction. They were not to be touched. I watched him lying there. There was not a sound from him for an hour, and then he began to moan.

'Nurse!' I called. 'Nurse!'

He obviously didn't know where he was or what had happened to him. His hands were at his throat, struggling to free himself. I could see the panic in his scratching fingers. He was crying out, in Polish I imagine, slurred, broken words.

Nurses came running, sisters. The matron of the ward bent over him, holding down his hands. 'You must not touch that harness!' she lectured him firmly. 'Do you understand? You have broken your neck! You have to lie perfectly still!' The Pole moaned weakly, those same broken words. I think he was still drunk.

His hands were bandaged, made into fingerless paddles. A nurse was instructed to sit by him, he had to be watched all the time. Then everyone else left. The ward quietened down. By now it must have been around eleven o'clock. The nurse sat there for another five minutes, and then she went for a walk.

This was Gloria, this nurse, the little pretty one with the dark eye make-up and the bouffant hair. She didn't go far, just three beds down on the other side of the aisle. There was a businessman there, in for tests, a rather smug fellow who had checked in that morning. In the quiet of the ward I could hear every word he said. We all could. He was confessing to Gloria the emptiness of his life. While pretty Gloria, no doubt, held his hand.

'I go to prostitutes,' his voice whispered out into the ward. 'I have to. My wife doesn't understand me. She never has, not from the very beginning. I don't know why I married her. I think I felt sorry for her. I mean, not for one minute has she given me what I really need.' On and on he went and it was all the same, all so predictable and trite, and in the middle of it the Pole, fighting to free himself of the harness around his neck with his useless hands, twisted somehow off the bed and fell to the floor.

He fell like a sack of sand.

Everyone heard it. It was impossible not to. The entire ward sprang instantly awake, bolt upright, wide-eyed. Nurses rushed, sisters, a flush-faced doctor in a dark chalk-striped suit. We saw him kneel by the Pole, rip open his pyjamas, plunge his ear to the thin white chest. The ward hung with horror. We could all see it. We could see it all. Then the curtain was pulled across.

'A cup of tea for everyone!' the head matron ordered, blazing down the aisle in her crimson cape. 'Relax, every-one! These things happen! Everything's under control!'

And the tea, of course, never came.

That was my last night at the New End. In the morning I was given a form to sign, my clothes, my bag. No one shook my hand, no one wished me luck, no one even said good-bye. I stepped out through the main entrance – the same doorway through which I had so blithely entered ten days ago – into a cold, grey, January day.

At once I was terrified of slipping, of falling over. The very air seemed too strong for me, too powerful. I felt dreadfully vulnerable, impossibly frail. I walked carefully down the hill, step by step, clutching my bag for dear life.

Passing Sainsburys I knew I should go in, I knew I should buy food, but I was too wonky, too frightened. I just wanted to get to my room. I wanted to be by myself. I wanted to sit down.

My key still miraculously unlocked the door.

Nothing had changed. It was just the same, exactly the same, the same foolishly cramped and crowded shoebox of a room. All that time at the New End it had been here, just like this, exactly the same. It seemed somehow miraculous, a revelation. I felt my eyes smarting, on the edge of tears.

I made myself some coffee on my impossibly slow hotplate, some biscuits and cheese. I eased myself down into my overstuffed armchair. There was mail to reply to, phonecalls to make, magazines to look at, books to read, a dozen and more things to do.

I sat.

I sat all afternoon, did nothing, wanted to do nothing, barely moved all afternoon. I looked through the window at the garden, the trees, the hedges, the light in the sky.

Just after six Katherine came, marvellous in her woolly coat, flushed and glowing. She flew into my arms, but then she drew back. 'How do you feel?' she said. 'Are you sure you should be standing up like this?'

And then Percival came, a few minutes later. He looked hesitant when he saw me with Katherine. 'Come in, come in!' I told him. 'There's plenty of room!'

Katherine ran upstairs to fetch water for more coffee – my room didn't boast that basic convenience. Then we sat around, we joked, we laughed, we talked.

We talked about the New End.

We talked about the nurses, the sisters, how crabby they all were, how the whole place was so rotten, a monument of uncaring, a black temple of stupidity and neglect. 'I had to wait two hours this morning,' I told them, 'just to get my clothes.' 'You're not at the Dorchester now!' Katherine mimicked, and we all laughed.

'And the food,' I said, and I told them how hungry I was all the time, and how I'd crept out of bed that night and found that stale piece of cake.

And I told them about the Pole, and how he'd died.

'Jesus,' Percival said.

We sat in maudlin silence, and then Katherine clapped her hands. 'Come on,' she said. 'I'm starving! What have you got to eat?'

'Well, not much,' I said, and then I remembered, and out of my bag I produced Katherine's tiny quail.

'My God, it's a sparrow!' Percival cried. 'We're going to eat a sparrow!'

Out of its jar it looked even more tiny, a naked and pitiful thing. Katherine divided it scrupulously, exactly into thirds. It was the merest mouthful each.

'How sad,' Katherine said, looking at the fragile bones.

And then we had more coffee and biscuits and cheese and then it was late and Percival went home and Katherine and I were at last alone. I put my arms around her. We softly kissed. For a long time we stood together in the centre of the room. 'Come to bed,' I said. 'Are you sure?' Katherine said, drawing back her head to look at me, to look into my eyes. 'Are you sure it's all right?' 'Come to bed,' I said.

O Swinging London, O miraculous days. In bed I held her in my arms and felt her never closer, never before such need, and in that instant when my heart flew out – my entire life, it seemed, my very soul – for a swooning moment I thought it would never return, I spun in endless blackness, I was surely lost, but then it did, and I felt a great peace settling over me, a wonderful warmth. I smiled. I rejoiced. I was alive.